Also by Maurine F. Dahlberg

Play to the Angel
The Spirit and Gilly Bucket

ESCAPE TO WEST BERLIN

ESCAPE|TO
WEST BERLIN

MAURINE F. DAHLBERG

Farrar, Straus and Giroux / *New York*

www.fsgkidsbooks.com

Library of Congress Cataloging-in-Publication Data
Dahlberg, Maurine F., date.
    Escape to West Berlin / Maurine F. Dahlberg.— 1st ed.
        p.   cm.
    Summary: In 1961 East Berlin, thirteen-year-old Heidi copes with the
stress of a crisis with her best friend, government pressure on her father to
leave his West Berlin job, her mother's pregnancy, and the ever-present
threat of the closing of the border with West Berlin.
    ISBN-13: 978-0-374-30959-6
    ISBN-10: 0-374-30959-0
    1. Berlin (Germany)—History—1945–1990—Juvenile fiction.
[1. Berlin (Germany)—History—1945–1990—Fiction.   2. Cold war—
Fiction.]   I. Title.

PZ7.D15157Ev 2004
[Fic]—dc22

2003053682

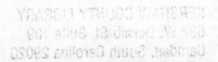

In memory of my grandmother
Leah Maude Fairchild,
who, like Oma,
loved flowers

ESCAPE TO
WEST BERLIN

1

"I KNOW THE TWO OF YOU CAN'T GO, but I can go by myself," I whispered.

I was standing at our living room window, looking out at the dull, rainy East Berlin evening and rehearsing the words I'd say to my parents. "You have no idea how much I look forward to going every year!"

I frowned. Those words didn't adequately describe the way I felt about our visits to my step-grandfather's farm. I loved every minute of every day there: sitting up in bed and watching the sun rise; having eggs, milk, fresh bread, and real butter for breakfast; helping Oma, my grandmother, work in the garden while she told me stories of her life during the war; riding Marta, Opa Fritz's gentle old horse.

My parents and I had gone to the farm every August that I could remember. But this August we couldn't go, because Mutter's doctors said that my new brother or sister would be born then.

Until last night, we had still planned to go to the farm. If the baby came early, Mutter had reasoned, old Dr. Klein in nearby Alt Mittelheim could deliver it. He was a friend of Oma and Opa Fritz's, and he'd delivered most of the young people on their farm cooperative. My parents liked and trusted him. But yesterday we had gotten a letter from Oma saying that Dr. Klein had suffered a stroke and couldn't work anymore. If the baby came early, Mutter would have to go to another town, farther away, to a doctor she didn't know. She and Vater had talked it over and finally, late last night, decided to cancel our trip. "I'm sorry, Heidi," Mutter had said. "We'll go next year." I'd replied, "Yes, Mutter," then cried into my pillow half the night. I didn't want my mother to be in any danger—but how could I bear not to go to the farm?

This morning I'd awakened with a brilliant idea in my head: I could go alone! "After all, I'll turn thirteen next week," I'd said excitedly to my best friend, Petra Hansen, "and I know where to change trains."

Petra had been skeptical. "My parents would never let me travel alone," she'd replied, shaking her head. Nevertheless, she had helped me list the reasons Mutter and Vater should let me go, and coached me as I practiced the speech I'd make to them tonight at dinner.

"Is it still raining, Heidi?" my mother asked, coming into the living room. Usually she was slender, like me, but these days she waddled like a duck on the Spree River.

"It's drizzling," I replied, lifting my dark, heavy hair. In this heat, it clung to the back of my neck like damp wool. I'd thought of cutting it short, but Petra said that it made me look like Jackie Kennedy, the American President's wife. Jackie Kennedy was the most glamorous woman we knew of, except maybe for my aunt Adelheide, Vater's younger sister, who lived in Munich, West Germany, and was an airline stewardess for Pan American Airlines. I was named for her.

Mutter picked up a magazine and fanned herself with it. "I wish we'd have one good storm that would cool things off instead of this constant rain. I think your father's right: July 1961 will go on record as the hottest-ever month in Berlin."

"Maybe so," I said thoughtfully. That was another reason for me to go to Opa Fritz's farm, I thought. It would be much cooler there than in the city. "Mutter, I have something important to ask you and Vater over dinner."

"Sounds mysterious." She smiled. "Do I get a hint beforehand?"

"No. I want to ask you both at once."

"Okay. Your father should be home any time now.

Would you set the table, please? Little Franzi wants me to put my feet up for a minute."

Little Franzi was what we were calling the baby. If it was a boy, his name would be Franz Dieter, for Vater and *his* father, who'd died in World War II; if it was a girl, her name would be Franziska Anne, for Vater and Mutter.

I went into the kitchen and got three blue-flowered plates out of the cupboard. They were part of a set that had belonged to Mutter's family. Mutter had told me that during the war she and her mother had packed the china and other breakables in straw-filled barrels and left them in the basement of their Berlin home while the family went to stay with cousins in the safer countryside. They'd come back to find their house partly destroyed by bombs, but the breakables were still nestled in the straw, waiting for the war to end.

When I crossed the hall to the living room to set the plates on the table, I saw that Mutter wasn't putting her feet up. She was standing at the living room window just as I had been, holding the lace curtain aside so she could see the street below.

"Is Vater coming?" I asked her.

"Not yet. You know how he forgets the time when he's working on cars."

I nodded, but I could see the worry lines in her forehead. Did she think something might have happened to Vater? I knew that she worried about his working across the border in West Berlin. I worried, too.

In school, we had learned why Berlin was divided into East and West. Back in 1945, when Germany lost the war, the four main winners divided it up: the Soviet Union took East Germany; the United States, Great Britain, and France took West Germany. Even though Berlin was in the middle of East Germany, it was split the same way: East Berlin was given to the Soviet Union; West Berlin, to the others.

Since then our leaders had been making East Germany, and East Berlin, into an ideal socialist society modeled on the Soviet Union: the government owned all the farms, factories, and stores, and in return gave everyone a job, low rent, and free schools and hospitals. Someday, when the system had been perfected, we would all share equally and live in peace and prosperity. But, as our leaders often said, it took time to build an ideal society. Meanwhile, the East was poor and shabby. Many people were growing impatient and leaving—even though they knew they'd be imprisoned if they got caught, since leaving the East was forbidden. Many other people, like Vater, were "border crossers," who had jobs over in wealthy West Berlin instead of here.

Just last week I had heard one of our government

leaders give a speech on the radio about the border crossers. "They take the benefits we provide, yet they're also earning high salaries working in the West!" he'd shouted. "We will soon be forced to take severe measures against them!" I didn't know what "severe measures" were, but after hearing that speech, I'd begun to worry about Vater.

"Your father probably had a last-minute customer," Mutter said. I wasn't sure whether she was trying to convince me or herself. "Hurry and finish setting the table. He'll be hungry when he gets home."

I brought out the glasses and flatware, and set three places at the table. I hoped our government wouldn't make Vater quit his job. He'd worked at Heinrich Sterns's Auto Shop from the time the war ended, before anybody knew that it would someday cause trouble to live in East Berlin and work in West Berlin. He was such a talented mechanic that many customers asked for him. "Herr Klenk knows what's wrong with a car just by listening to it!" one man had raved. Vater liked Herr Sterns and the men he worked with, and he often told us how modern and well stocked the shop was.

While I was putting out the napkins, cutting board, and bread knife, the mantel clock on the living room shelf struck seven. *Bong-bong,* it said in deep, important tones. Like the china plates, it had spent the war packed in Mutter's family's basement. When it *bonged*, I liked to pretend that it was saying my family's names.

First came "Karl Franz!" and "Anne-marie!" for my parents, then "Hei-di!" for me. After our names came "Frie-drich!" for Opa Fritz, "So-phie!" for Oma, and "Adel-heide!" for my aunt. Next was "Die-ter!" for Oma's first husband, Vater's father, who'd been killed in the last days of the war, when the young boys and old men had been the only ones left to fight. If I was awake at midnight, I'd also "hear" the names of my other relatives who had died before I was born: Mutter's father and three brothers, who, like Opa Dieter, had been killed in the war, and her mother, who had died of cancer. Soon I would have to add "Fran-zi!" for the baby. But where? I already had twelve people.

Just as the seventh *bong-bong*, the one for Opa Dieter, was fading away, Mutter turned from the window.

"He's here!" she cried, her face glowing with relief and happiness. "He's coming up the walk. Unlock the front door so he doesn't have to stand out in the rain."

I ran into the entryway and pressed the button that unlocked the door to our building. Then I opened our apartment door and listened to Vater whistling as he came upstairs.

I loved that moment, I thought, when Vater got home and we were all together.

Mutter pushed past me with her baby-stomach and stood in the doorway. "Karl Franz, you're late!"

He said, "I stayed to talk to Heinrich Sterns."

I saw Mutter raise her eyebrows and Vater nod. What was that about? I wondered.

After Vater got inside, my parents exchanged a hug and kiss, then Vater winked at me. "Heidi, are you too grown-up to say hello to your father?"

"Well, not quite," I teased. I gave him a kiss, the way I always did. Unlike Mutter, who was nearly as tall as Vater, I had to stand on my tiptoes to do it. His black hair and blue workshirt smelled of the auto shop. I liked the smell because it was his.

Once the door was closed, I asked, "You didn't have any trouble with the border police, did you? Coming home?"

"No, none at all. Were you worried?"

"A little," I confessed.

"Well, don't worry anymore." He grinned as we went into the living room. "The government might not like my working in the West, but they can't stop me. It isn't illegal. Now tell me, how is your first week of summer vacation going?"

"Fine." I added happily, "No more school until the first of September! That's still more than a month away."

Vater said, "I'm sorry we can't go to the farm this year. You won't get bored staying home, will you?"

"It depends," I replied slowly. "I've thought of something I want to do on my vacation. I'll tell you and Mutter about it over supper."

"We'll be all ears," he promised, and went to wash up.

I poured orange soda into our glasses while Mutter set the food on the table: canned sausage, canned beets, half a loaf of bread, a small block of cheese, and sliced tomatoes from our garden plot. Hooray for our garden, I thought gratefully. Without the tomatoes, this would have been just another sacrifice-for-tomorrow supper.

That was what I called the meager meals we often had, because our government leaders said the food shortage was one of the sacrifices we were making for a better tomorrow. I tried to be patient, and I was proud of helping to build our new society—but it was hard to eat our dreary little meals when just over in West Berlin you could get oranges and bananas and bottles of Coca-Cola. Occasionally we were able to sneak something across the border to bring home, but if we got caught, the East German border guards would take it away. "Probably so they can eat and drink it themselves," Petra often grumbled.

After we'd sat down, Vater sliced the loaf. We all

took some bread, and cheese, and sausage, and helped ourselves to the tomatoes and beets. As we ate, Vater told us about his day: he'd figured out a tricky problem with a carburetor; he'd gotten to service a gorgeous new Mercedes; and he'd had to scold Arno, the apprentice, for hiding a rubber snake in the new bookkeeper's desk drawer and making her scream. Finally he said, "What were you going to tell us about your vacation, Heidi?"

I put down my fork, cleared my throat, and began reciting the words I'd rehearsed: "I know the two of you can't go to Opa Fritz's. But I love the farm, and I'll die if I can't go there this year!" I reminded them that I'd be thirteen next week and that I'd gone to the farm every summer of my life.

"But you've always gone with *us*. You can't be thinking of traveling all the way to Alt Mittelheim by yourself," Mutter protested.

"I can certainly go alone." If I hadn't been trying to sound reasonable and grown-up, I would have stamped my foot in frustration. "I know exactly what to do. Listen: I get on the train here at the East Berlin station. It's number fifty-four, it's called the Vindobona, and it leaves at nine-oh-eight every morning. Here are the towns it goes through: Zossen, Uckro, Doberlug-Kirchhain, Elsterwerda, Grossenhain, Radebeul, Dresden."

My parents looked surprised that I knew so much.

I continued. "When I get to Dresden, I catch the train to Tharandt. I get off in Freital and take the local train to Alt Mittelheim. When I get there, I wait at the station for Opa Fritz to come. I mustn't leave my raincoat on the train, I mustn't talk to strangers, and I must always cooperate with the transport police."

Vater laughed. "Very good!"

I nodded eagerly. "See? I can do it. And I won't go until the middle of August, when you're on vacation. That way Mutter won't be alone all day."

"I don't know, Heidi," Mutter said. "What if you got sick? Or what if you went to sleep and didn't get off the train in Dresden? You'd end up in—"

"Vienna, Austria," I supplied promptly. "That's the end of the line for the Vindobona. But I wouldn't get that far. The border police would wake me up and throw me off the train at the Czech border."

My parents looked at each other. Their eyes asked, "Shall we let her go?"

Then Vater turned to me and shook his head. "I'm sorry, sweetheart. Another time it would be all right, but we have too much on our minds now, with the baby coming."

I swallowed hard and looked down at my plate.

"Besides," Vater continued, "things are tense in East Germany. Thousands of people have fled West this summer, because of the food shortage over here and the government's threats to us border crossers. I've heard there are four times as many transport police as usual on the trains and subways, to try to catch people who are defecting to the West."

"But I wouldn't be defecting. Why would they bother me?"

"They're bothering everybody. It isn't a good time for you to go alone."

"Your father is right," Mutter said. "We'd worry about you the whole time."

I had one more argument, the one Petra had thought was the best. "Oma said in her last letter that she's worried about Opa Fritz's heart. What if he—I mean, what if something happens and I never get to see him again?"

Vater merely said, "Oma has always been worried about Opa Fritz's heart. Even Dr. Klein couldn't get him to slow down or take the heart medicine he needs. Opa Fritz is in no more danger now than he's been in for years." He brightened. "I'll tell you what. After the baby's born, you and I can go to the farm for a weekend. How will that be?"

"Fine," I murmured. Going for a weekend wouldn't be a real vacation.

"Heidi—" Mutter began.

"It's all right," I said quickly. If we kept talking about the farm, I'd burst into tears.

We were quiet for the rest of the meal. When we'd finished eating, I helped Mutter clear the table, then went to my tiny bedroom, which opened off the living room.

Max, my stuffed toy gorilla, smiled sweetly at me from his perch on my pillow, and I picked him up and hugged him. He had been mine since my fifth birthday, when Oma and Opa Fritz had given him to me. He knew all my secrets. He saw all the hairstyles I tried in front of the mirror, he watched me experiment with Mutter's makeup, he heard me swear under my breath whenever I had trouble with my homework, and he knew how much I liked rock-and-roll music. He even knew that I still had nightmares about swimming because I had almost drowned last June. Sometimes, like now, he saw me cry.

"It's not fair, Max," I whispered bitterly. "I didn't ask for a brother or sister, but I'm getting one, anyway, and it's ruining *every*thing. We can't go to the farm, and we never get to go to the movies or spend weekends in the garden cottage anymore. Besides, I'll have to share my room, and there's hardly enough space in here for *me*."

I smoothed the top of Max's head. I had been crying

on him so much lately I was almost surprised his fur wasn't growing, as plants do after it rains. The thought of his plush head-fur getting longer and longer made me laugh. "I'd have to trim it," I told him, "or you'd look like the hoodlums we see over in West Berlin."

His face seemed puzzled and a little hurt.

"Sorry, Max. I shouldn't laugh at you," I said. But I did feel better.

I brushed away a tear from my cheek. Then I put Max back on my pillow and turned on my radio, as I always did after supper. Evening was when I could tune in the Western European stations. I had to keep the volume low so our neighbors wouldn't hear. It was forbidden to listen to Western radio stations here in the East. Our government said they played indecent music and told lies about us. But I listened to them, anyway; I loved rock and roll, and the best songs were from America, England, and West Germany. Although I couldn't understand all the English words, I didn't think the songs were indecent. They were mostly about love and broken hearts. As for the lies, I didn't listen to the news broadcasts, and wouldn't have understood the ones in English.

I put my ear up close to the radio. My favorite station, the British one in Luxembourg, was still faint and filled with static, so I turned the dial to the American Forces Network in West Berlin. Unlike Radio Luxembourg, it didn't play the very newest hits, but the reception was better.

The tuning eye on the radio turned a strong bright green, and Elvis Presley crooned a ballad about being lonely. I wasn't crazy about Elvis: his tight clothes and smoldering eyes made me uneasy. Still, his deep, velvety voice soothed my anger and disappointment, and soon I started to feel better about not getting to go to the farm. After all, I thought, my parents were having a hard time. It couldn't be easy for Mutter to be having a baby after all these years, and Vater must be anxious about the severe measures the government was threatening to take against the border crossers. Besides, maybe once my parents had Little Franzi to care for, they would treat me as more grown-up. Already they were letting me go out more on my own, since Mutter often needed me to shop and run errands for her.

When Elvis had finished, I gave a big sigh and turned off the radio.

"I'll be back," I told Max, setting him on my pillow.

The television was on in the living room, but Mutter and Vater weren't watching it. I knew they were probably in the kitchen, having a private conversation. Often they turned on the television, then went into the kitchen and talked softly. That way, if they wanted to criticize the government or say other things that might get them in trouble, the sound of the TV set would keep the neighbors from hearing them.

I crept into the entryway, next to the kitchen door. I was torn between wanting to respect my parents' privacy and wanting to let them know that I'd thought things over and understood why they didn't want me to go to the farm.

I had just decided to wait and talk to them later when I heard Mutter say, "Shall we tell Heidi?"

It was funny how such softly spoken words could hit you like a punch in the stomach. I stood as still as a statue, listening.

Vater was silent for a moment. "Not yet. Let's not burden her with it."

Mutter said, "All right. Now let's go watch TV and try to relax."

Quickly, before they saw me, I tiptoed back to my bedroom.

Burden me with *what*?

2

WHEN I WOKE UP THE NEXT MORNING, my clock said nine-thirty. I smiled to myself. It was lovely not to have to get up early and go to school.

"Good morning, Max," I said, reaching out to pat his nose with my finger. During the hot summers he spent the night on the bedside table instead of cuddled next to me.

Through the thin wall beside my bed, our neighbors, the Weppelmanns, were making their usual noises. The door of the wardrobe creaked open and shut, something was dropped and rolled heavily across the floor, and Herr Weppelmann coughed his smoker's hacking cough. Frau Weppelmann called to him from the kitchen, and he yelled back to say he couldn't hear her. I had heard her perfectly, and wondered what would happen if I banged on the wall and bellowed, "She asked you to fix the leak in the toilet!"

As my brain came awake, I started remembering things. Mutter and Vater had said I couldn't go to the farm. They'd said something else, too, something that had scared me. *Shall we tell Heidi? Not yet. Let's not burden her with it.*

I grabbed Max and lay there in bed, thinking. What could they have meant? Of course, with the way they tried to protect me, the burden might be very small. Maybe they just couldn't afford to give me a birthday present, or wanted me to do extra chores once the baby was born.

After a few minutes, I got up and went out to the living room, still in my pajamas. Mutter was at the dining table, eating breakfast. Last week she had started her year-long maternity leave from her job as an office manager at Humboldt University.

"Morning, Mutter," I said, and kissed her cheek. "Is the tea still hot?"

"It should be," she said. "I hope the television didn't wake you."

"No, the Weppelmanns did," I told her.

"Ah, so they're still alive," Mutter joked. We hardly ever saw the Weppelmanns, and when we did, they seldom spoke and never smiled. Tall, stooped old Herr Weppelmann would scowl from under his shaggy eyebrows and grunt in reply to our greetings. His small, timid wife would nod without lifting her eyes. Frau Ludwig, across the hall from us, said that they didn't always come to the door when she rang their bell, even though she could hear them inside. The Korths, upstairs, thought they were retired government spies. I didn't know what they were, but they gave me the creeps.

I poured myself a mug of tea and took it back to the table. Mutter had already set a place for me across from her. As I sat down, she pushed the bread and a jar of Oma's blackberry preserves over to me.

"What are your plans for the day?" she asked. "Are you doing something with the Pioneers?"

"Not today. There's a trip to the history museum, but I went there last spring."

The government-sponsored Pioneer organization was woven into our school lives and offered many activities during our vacations, as well. All my classmates belonged, except for the few who were Christians and joined church groups instead. We went on hikes, took day trips, camped out, attended programs and concerts, had parties, and did good-citizenship projects. Sometimes we had to listen to boring political lectures or watch films with titles such as *The Glorious Struggle for Socialism*, but usually we had fun. I had learned to swim through the Pioneers, and I had met Petra there when we were ten. Her family had just moved to our neighborhood and I thought she looked lonely, so I asked her to be my partner for our group's scrap-metal collection drive. We became friends right away.

Mutter and I ate silently, watching television. The news was the same as usual: the polio epidemic in the West was getting worse, but Easterners were safe; thousands of East German citizens had volunteered to spend their Sundays helping farmers bring in the harvest, in order to further the cause of peace and prosperity; and Herr Ulbricht, the leader of our government, had made a speech somewhere in Berlin. The camera showed him standing behind a podium as he addressed the crowd.

Looking at his prim face with its thin lips and rounded little beard, I giggled. "Herr Ulbricht looks like a sheep."

Mutter set down her cup so hard that the tea sloshed into the saucer.

"Be careful what you say! People have gone to prison for less than that!"

I stared at her, shocked. She'd never spoken to me that way before. "I'm sorry, Mutter."

She put a shaking hand to her forehead, and took a deep breath. "It's all right. I'm afraid I'm a bit jumpy these days."

"Is it because of—of the baby?" I had almost said "Because of that burden you don't want to put on me?"

"It's partly that." Mutter lowered her voice. "Also, I was watching the West Berlin station earlier, to get the Western version of the news. It said that nearly thirty thousand East Germans have registered at the refugee center this month."

"Thirty thousand! Do you think it's true?"

Mutter nodded slowly. "Like your father said, people are tired of the food shortages and the new restrictions over here. They want to be able to feed their families, to travel, to choose their own jobs, to vote for their leaders, and to tune in to Western TV and radio programs if they choose."

"But my Pioneer leaders say that the shortages and restrictions are only temporary," I told her. I felt very grown-up, drinking tea and discussing politics with Mutter. "They say that when we've finished building our new society, we'll have plenty of food and we won't need so many rules. Then people will be glad they stayed and made the sacrifices."

Mutter thought for a moment before she answered. "A lot of people think that we'll never have that wonderful new society—and that even if we do, it won't be worth the sacrifice of so much freedom."

"But in the Pioneers, we learn that people have too *much* freedom in the West. It leads to violence and poverty."

"Do you think so?"

"That's what we're told," I replied uncertainly.

When I was younger, I'd accepted everything our Pioneer leaders said. In many ways East Germany *was* a good place to live: our government made sure that we were cared for. No one was wealthy, but there was no poverty. Even though our meals were boring, there was always plenty of canned food in the stores. We never had riots or strikes, as the Western countries did. We supported peace, too, whereas our leaders said that the West loved to build weapons and wage war. Still, lately I had begun to tear apart the political lectures our Pioneer leaders gave us and to ask questions I didn't dare voice: Is it right to make people stay here and help build our new society if they don't want to? Is it right to treat us like prisoners, not allowing us to move away, or to travel to countries that aren't governed by the Soviet Union?

I confessed, "I don't always know what I think."

Mutter sighed. "I guess I don't either. At any rate, our government is certain to do something soon to stop people from leaving, and nobody knows what. Berlin's like a box of firecrackers, waiting for somebody to throw in a lighted match. We all have to be more careful than ever about what we say and do. That especially goes for you and me since your father works in the West. Understand?"

I nodded.

"Good." Mutter finished her tea. "Would you mind going to the milk shop and bakery this morning? We're out of milk, and nearly out of bread."

"Okay, I'll go as soon as I've gotten dressed." I knew from experience that the shops sold out quickly. If you didn't get there early, you'd come home empty-handed.

When Mutter gave me the money for the shops, she said, "Be sure to get the milk last, or it will spoil before you get home."

"Yes, Mutter." She told me that every time I went shopping, as though I had no more sense than a goose.

I put on a sleeveless top and cotton shorts, but I was sweating before I got to the end of our block. Berlin felt like one of the African jungles or South American rain forests we'd studied in school. I couldn't help thinking how much cooler it would be at Opa Fritz's farm.

The line at the bakery shuffled along slowly, and I was thankful when I finally had the plump, crusty loaf in my hands.

"All we need now is butter to put on our bread," a woman murmured to me as we left the shop. "The West Germans offered to send us some, but Herr Ulbricht was too proud to accept."

I remembered Mutter's words about being careful. "I'm sure our leaders know best," I replied, and quickly walked away from her.

The milk shop line moved faster, but it was nearly noon before I started home. On our district's main street, some members of the Free German Youth—which was like the Pioneers, but for older kids—were putting up posters on the drab apartment buildings. SOCIALISM IS TRIUMPHING! WE ARE THE STRONGER! the bold type proclaimed. Others said OUR DEEDS STRENGTHEN EAST GERMANY! There was a whole line of identical posters with a picture of Herr Ulbricht and the words WALTER ULBRICHT, OUR LEADER! A MAN FOR PEACE AND PROSPERITY! Looking at them, I remembered how Mutter had snapped at me earlier. But Herr Ulbricht *did* look like a sheep, and I had to stifle a giggle because the line of posters looked like a whole flock of sheep standing in a row and bleating at passersby.

"Heidi, wait!" a familiar voice called. I turned and saw Petra running across the street from the subway stop. Like me, she wore shorts, and her gym bag bumped against her tanned, skinny legs. I waved, and waited for her to catch up.

"Hi!" She brushed some short, blond tendrils of hair from her forehead. "Did you ask your parents about going to the farm?"

I scowled. "They said no. They said they have enough on their minds, with the baby coming."

"I'm sorry," Petra said sympathetically. "I know you love going there."

We started walking down the street. The Hansens lived in a big apartment house a few blocks from us, in the same direction.

"Where have you been?" I asked, nodding at her gym bag.

"The pool, with Ulrike Eisenstein."

I grunted. Pretty, silky-haired Ulrike was the model our teachers and Pioneer leaders held up to the rest of us. She was our class's representative to the Friendship Council, which led the school's Pioneer program, and was always winning prizes for her schoolwork and leadership. She was friendly enough, but I didn't like her cool, superior smile, or the way her gray eyes seemed to look right through people. I especially didn't like her habit of quoting from the Pioneer rule book.

"You seem to be spending a lot of time with Ulrike lately," I said sourly to Petra.

She shrugged. "My father got transferred to a new office recently, and Herr Eisenstein is one of his directors. He thought it would be nice for me to be friends with Ulrike. Besides," she added, "she likes to swim and *you* won't go to the pool with me anymore."

"I don't like to leave Mutter alone for that long," I replied stiffly.

Petra nodded knowingly. "And you're still scared of swimming, aren't you?"

I shrugged and didn't answer.

"Heidi, you need to get over your fear! You used to love to swim, and you were good at it—the best in our Pioneer swimming class. It would be a shame for you never to get back in the water."

"I'll probably swim again someday," I said. "Just not now."

"It will only get harder the longer you wait," Petra argued. "You should go swimming in the pool, where you know you'll be safe, so you can get used to being in the water again. Then, when we go to the Müggelsee next month, you won't be scared anymore. You *are* coming, since you're not going to the farm?"

The Müggelsee was a huge lake near East Berlin. The Pioneers from my class had gone there on a day trip in June, and decided to go again in late August.

I shook my head firmly. "I'm not going to the Müggelsee."

Petra looked at me in astonishment. "You're not going? Oh, Heidi, don't say that! You'll be fine as long as you stay near the shore with the rest of us."

"No!" I said firmly. "I'm not going back there. I

don't ever want to see the Müggelsee again, and I don't want to talk about it."

We walked a ways without saying anything. We'd never quarreled until lately. We'd already had three arguments this summer. Two had been over my not swimming. The other had been about the government. We'd been walking home from a Pioneer lecture and I'd tried to express my confusion. If East Germany truly was the Workers' Paradise, I'd said, we shouldn't have to force workers to stay here. Petra's eyes had gotten wide, and she'd whispered that I shouldn't say such things. I'd kept talking, and she'd covered her ears and refused to listen.

I cleared my throat. "Do you still want to go to the West Berlin zoo on my birthday?"

To my relief, Petra grinned. "Of course I do! And we're going to stop at a café for coffee and cake, too."

"Yes, to celebrate my becoming a *teeeenager*." I drew out the word the way the American rock-and-roll singers did. We both giggled, and the awkward feeling between us was gone.

When we got to the corner where Petra turned and I went straight, she said, "I wish you'd change your mind about coming to the Müggelsee. It's going to be a lot of fun."

"I'll think about it," I murmured, knowing I wouldn't. "Bye, Petra!"

"Bye. See you at the park this Sunday!"

"I'll be there." We had signed up on the Pioneers' volunteer list to trim the flowers and pick up trash at the local park.

As I walked on home, I thought about what Petra had said. I *had* been the best swimmer in our class, and it had nearly cost me my life in June. Frau Hoffmann, our Pioneer leader, had told us to stay close to the shore of the lake, but I'd figured that didn't apply to Heidi Klenk, Star Swimmer.

I was fine until the water became choppy. Then, as I turned my head to take a breath, I was slapped in the face by a wave and gulped down water instead of air. I started choking and coughing, and suddenly the sparkling blue lake seemed powerful and menacing, and the shore a very long way off. I panicked. This is what it's like to drown, I thought as I flailed helplessly. And I *would* have drowned if Frau Hoffmann hadn't seen me and come to my rescue. She turned me on my back, crooked her arm under my chin, and swam me back to shore.

As a punishment for disobeying her orders, Frau Hoffmann made me stay out of the water for the rest of the day. It was hardly a punishment, though, because I had no wish to go into the lake again.

Afterward, she came home with me and told my

parents what had happened. To my relief, she just said I'd swum too far out, and didn't say that I had disobeyed her. I guessed she knew I was too shaken ever to take such a risk again. Mutter brought me supper in bed that evening, and sympathized when I told her how scared I had been. Then, that night, I woke her and Vater after I had a nightmare about drowning. Mutter fixed me a cup of warm milk to drink, and Vater sat with me until I went back to sleep.

But Max was the only one who knew that I still had nightmares. I didn't want anyone else to know. After all, I could hardly convince Mutter and Vater that I was growing up and could do things on my own if I kept waking them to come sit with me. And if Petra found out I still had nightmares, she would insist that I get over my fear by swimming again. She didn't understand that I would *never* swim again. Even now, walking home on a hot, sunny day, I shuddered at the thought of being in the lake or even in the local swimming pool.

When I got home, I put the jug of milk in the refrigerator and the loaf of bread in the cupboard. Mutter and I had a can of goulash for lunch. Then we listened to a classical music program on the radio while we cleaned the living room.

When we took a break, Mutter rubbed her back

and said, "Would you go get the mail? It should be here by now. I'm afraid Little Franzi doesn't want to go up and down the steps today."

"Okay." I got the mailbox key from the kitchen drawer, where we kept it, and hurried down the stairs to the front entryway. I hoped there'd be a postcard from Aunt Adelheide. She was on a month-long vacation in America with some of her stewardess friends. They were taking the train down the East Coast from New York City to Florida, and she'd promised to send me postcards to add to my collection. Over the years, she'd sent me postcards from all around the world, and I kept them in an old jewelry box of Mutter's.

But today there was no postcard in our mailbox, just a government flyer warning us to beware of Western spies and a letter for Vater. The return address on the letter was our district's town hall. What could the town hall want with Vater?

It was probably just a routine letter, I told myself as I went slowly back up the stairs. Maybe the rent was being raised or there was a new regulation for us to follow. But I kept thinking of the words I'd heard on the radio in the speech about border crossers: *We will soon be forced to take severe measures against them!*

"Vater got a letter from the town hall," I told Mutter.

"The town hall? Let me see." I held out the envelope. I watched her face, but I couldn't tell anything from her expression. Finally she said, "Put it on the coffee table, and your father will open it when he gets home."

"Do you think it's bad news?" I asked her.

I hoped she'd say, "Oh, it's nothing. Don't worry so much!" But instead she hesitated and then said, "We can't know until he reads it."

Vater got home early that evening. Mutter opened the door for him, and after they'd exchanged kisses, I heard her say, "You got a letter from the town hall."

I watched anxiously as he stood in the living room and read it. He scowled, put it back in the envelope, and stuffed it into his pocket.

"What do they want?" I asked.

"Oh, they just want me to go there for an appointment on Monday," he replied offhandedly. "It's probably for another lecture on how disloyal I am to work in the West."

"They can't—well, arrest you or anything, can they?"

He ruffled my hair. "No, they can't arrest me. I've told you before, working in the West isn't against the law. They just want to harass me."

I felt reassured. Vater was right: he wasn't doing anything illegal. Besides, there were fifty thousand or more border crossers. The government couldn't possibly arrest that many people! Where would it put them?

We had another sacrifice-for-tomorrow supper: bowls of watery canned vegetable soup and rolls spread with funny-tasting margarine.

"Aren't there any more tomatoes?" I asked.

Mutter shook her head. "We finished them last night."

"Tomorrow," Vater said to me, "you and I can go out to the garden. A lot more tomatoes should be ripe by now, and there are probably some beans, carrots, and cabbages ready, too."

I grinned, and not just at the thought of having fresh food. Next to Opa Fritz's farm, the garden plot we rented was my favorite place in the world. It was in south East Berlin, near where the Teltow Canal formed the border with West Berlin. The whole area was a neighborhood of tiny fenced-in gardens, each with its own gate opening off a gravel path. Like the other gardens, ours had a little cottage in it, where we often spent summer weekends when we weren't at Opa Fritz's. Or we *had*, up until this summer. Because of Little Franzi, Mutter had seldom felt like it this year.

After I'd helped wash the dishes, I went to my room to listen to the radio. The British station in Luxembourg came in clearly, but when I heard one of the Weppelmanns come into their bedroom next door, I had to turn the volume so low I could barely hear it.

I put my radio on the floor and lay down with my ear next to it. That way I could hear the tunes, if not the words. And the words didn't matter, since I couldn't understand most of them, anyway—just the ones that were used a lot: *love, lonesome, heart, baby, teenager, stars,* and *goodbye.*

"I love you, baby," I whispered to Max in English, and giggled.

After a while I heard the television come on in the living room. I could tell from the narrator's emotionless, singsong voice that the TV was tuned to the East Berlin station. That surprised me because my parents watched mostly the Western stations, which had better programs, with the volume turned low. I wondered what was on the East Berlin station tonight that was so interesting.

I got my answer later, when I passed through the living room on my way to the bathroom. The program was about an industrial plant that was celebrating its fifth anniversary. But Mutter and Vater weren't watching it. They weren't even in the living room. I knew without looking that they were in the kitchen, whispering again about that mysterious burden.

3

When I went into the living room the next morning, Vater was dressed in his work clothes and gulping down a cup of coffee. "I need to go to the shop for a little while," he said. "I'll be home before noon and we can visit the garden then."

"Okay. But how come you have to work? You're usually off Saturday mornings."

"I won't be working this morning. Heinrich and I just have some things to talk over. Now I'd better get a move on."

He set his cup on the table, kissed the top of my head, and left. I stared after him, thinking. He and Herr Sterns seemed to be talking a lot these days. Could their talks have anything to do with the burden my parents had mentioned?

When he got home, we had an early lunch. Then

we said goodbye to Mutter and set off for the garden. It took about half an hour to get there. We had to take the subway to the Alexanderplatz stop, catch the city train to the Plänterwald station, and walk several blocks to the garden.

I was so eager to get to the garden that I tugged at my father's hand as we walked the last block. "Hurry, Vater!"

He chuckled and began walking a little faster. "I think you've inherited your grandmother's love of gardening."

It pleased me to think I was taking after Oma. Of course, you could hardly be around Oma and *not* catch her passion for gardening. She worked in the wheat fields, along with the other members of the government-owned farm cooperative, and she helped Opa Fritz in the vegetable garden, but her flower garden was her real love. She'd say, "Fritz grumbles that we need the space for more vegetables, but I put my foot down. People need beauty for their souls as much as they need food for their stomachs, especially after the ugliness of the war."

Many people seemed to agree with her, because they came for miles to look at her garden. Often we would see cars creep down the road and stop so that the passengers could admire the colorful tapestry made by the flowers: the rows of bold scarlet, orange, and magenta zinnias; the tall cream, pink, and salmon snapdragon spires; the masses of deep ruby and garnet pansies; the dark purple petunias; the russet and lemon marigolds; and the giant sunflowers that stood high over them all.

It seemed as if everyone in East Berlin who had a garden was working in it that day. When we turned down our path, I waved to old Herr Hartz, who had the plot next to ours. He usually looked after our garden while we were at Opa Fritz's, in return for some of our potatoes and cabbages at harvesttime.

"Good afternoon!" he called, and came over to the fence. "Won't you folks be leaving for vacation soon?"

Vater shook his head. "I'm afraid we can't go this year. The baby is due in a few weeks, so we had to cancel our trip."

While they stood at the fence and talked, I got the tools out of the tall storage cabinet that adjoined the cottage. I wished Vater hadn't mentioned the baby. I didn't want to think about Little Franzi today. I just wanted to enjoy working in the garden.

We watered, weeded, and clipped dead flowers. Then Vater picked beans while I tidied the cottage. We hadn't stayed there in a long time, and it smelled musty. I put up the blinds and opened the windows to let in some fresh air while I swept, dusted, and knocked away the cobwebs. There was a spiderweb in the corner by my cot that was so perfect I let it be. The spider and her children would be long gone by the time we were able to spend a weekend here again.

When I'd finished, I helped Vater with the beans. We got a small pail of them—enough for at least two meals. In a basket we put six carrots, a fat purple cabbage, six big scarlet tomatoes, and lots of deep-green spinach leaves. What a treasure!

I stuck the trowel and clippers down in the basket and tucked my gardening gloves under the cabbage. "I have to help the Pioneers clean up the park tomorrow," I explained to Vater.

Mutter had bought some sausage at the butcher's, so supper that night was cooked cabbage with chunks of sausage in it, and sliced tomatoes. With the beans, carrots, spinach, and remaining tomatoes, we would have good suppers until it was time for our next trip to the garden. I loved this time of year, when we had fresh food that we'd planted and grown ourselves.

When I got to our local park the next day, kids from my Pioneer group were already at work. I looked around and saw Petra, Ulrike Eisenstein, Karin Metzger, and Dagmar Reinhardt weeding a plot of red and white petunias. I scowled. I didn't want to work with Ulrike, but I knew that Petra was expecting me.

"Ah, here's a real gardener!" chubby, red-haired

Dagmar cried as I joined them. At school, Dagmar helped me in math and I helped her in gardening class. I sometimes teased her about how she could work complex math problems yet have trouble telling carrot and radish seedlings apart.

"Hello, Heidi." Karin tucked her long blond hair behind her ears. She looked surprised to see me. "I thought you'd be at your grandparents' farm. Don't you usually go there in August?"

"We can't go this year because my mother is having a baby," I replied, slipping on my gardening gloves. I looked at the petunias. "Where shall I start?"

Petra pointed with her weed digger. "There, in the middle. We began at the ends, so we'll be working toward you."

As we worked, we chatted about the upcoming school term, the kids we'd talked to lately, our vacation plans, and the International Children's Festival, which East Berlin would be hosting in August. Soon the others began talking about the Müggelsee trip—how much fun it would be, what games they wanted to play, and what food was planned for the picnic.

I tugged on a stubborn weed, suddenly feeling irritable. What was so wonderful about going to the Müggelsee?

Ulrike looked at me. "Heidi, are you going?"

"No, I don't think so."

"Oh, but you have to!" Dagmar protested. "Everybody's going."

Karin asked, "You aren't scared after what happened last time, are you? When you swam too far out?"

"You don't have to swim if you don't want to," Dagmar put in. "You can just play volleyball and lie in the sun."

I shook my head. "I don't think I want to go."

Ulrike's gray eyes regarded me coolly. "If you do as our leaders say, you'll be fine. Last time, you disobeyed the rules, and that's why you got into trouble."

I was furious. How dare she lecture me like that?

"I don't want to go!" I snapped. "I'm tired of hearing about it, and I'm tired of rules!"

Ulrike raised her eyebrows. "But our society is based on rules. It's our duty to follow them. Pioneers are respectful and well disciplined, remember?"

Petra shot me a nervous glance. Karin and Dagmar kept their heads bowed over their work, but I sensed their tension. I thought of how much trouble Ulrike could cause for my family if she told our Pioneer leaders about my outburst. They might even have someone spy on us to see whether my parents were also tired of rules.

I made myself smile at her. "Don't mind me. I know it's important to do what our leaders say. I'm just out of sorts because I can't go to the farm this summer."

Petra quickly added, "I can see why Heidi wouldn't want to go on the Müggelsee trip. After all, her little brother or sister might be born that day!"

I gave her a grateful smile. "That's right. The baby is due about then, and I'd be worried about my mother the whole time."

Ulrike smiled graciously and said, "Of course, Heidi. I understand."

I wanted to tell her I didn't care whether she understood. Even more, I wanted to fill my trowel with soil and go dump it on her long, shiny brown hair. *That* would wipe the smirk off her face, especially if there were plenty of fat, juicy earthworms to wriggle down her neck.

Monday was the day of Vater's appointment at the town hall. He didn't get back until nearly six. "What happened?" Mutter asked as soon as he'd shut the door behind him.

"It was pretty much what I'd expected," he said, taking off his coat. He hung it on a hook in the hallway. "They tried to get me to sign a paper saying I'd give up my job and get one in the East. I reminded them that this isn't a good time to be looking for work, since a lot of employers are on vacation in August. They agreed to give me until the tenth of September to find something. That means I'd better start looking tomorrow."

The next morning, he left early to start his job search. He came home late that afternoon, with a grim face.

"No luck?" Mutter asked.

He motioned for us to go into the kitchen, our safe place to talk. Then he said, "I got offers from two garages."

"You did?" I cried. "Are you going to accept one?"

He hesitated. "I told both of the foremen I'd let them know. I hope I don't have to take either of them. One garage had rats the size of Opa Fritz's barn cats, and standing water in the shop area because the drain-pipes were too small. At the other, I'd have to attend socialist lectures every morning before work. At both, I'd get paid less than half of what I make at Heinrich's. At the second one, I'd be replacing a man who was fired because he asked for a raise. Both garages had al-most no spare parts, and the mechanics said they were short of tools and equipment as well. They said they spent most of their time looking for tools and car parts on the black market."

"Surely you'll find something better," I said.

He sighed. "I hope so. In the meantime, if people ask, say I've had two offers."

That was all he would tell us. Over supper, he and Mutter talked about baby furniture. Later, we were sitting on the couch watching television, and between programs I turned to him and said, "Vater, I'm sorry you have to get a new job. If—if you'd rather not spend the money, we can skip my birthday dinner tomorrow evening."

"Thanks, sweetheart, but we still have plenty of money." He winked at me. "Besides, I'm looking forward to it. Have you decided where you want to go?"

We discussed various West Berlin restaurants we liked: the Radio Tower had good food and a view of all Berlin, Kranzler's had wonderful pastries, Kottler's had large servings and a man who played the zither while you ate, and Café Vienna was sophisticated and elegant.

I finally decided on the Radio Tower. Vater said, "Okay. I'll call tomorrow and reserve a table on the western side so we can watch the sun set."

Someone who didn't know Vater would have thought he had nothing more important on his mind than where to take his daughter for dinner. But to me, his face looked tired and strained and his voice was a little *too* carefree. And once again he and Mutter stayed in the kitchen and whispered until late at night.

When I woke up the next morning, I reached for Max. "I'm thirteen now!" I told him happily.

At breakfast, there were cards and gaily wrapped presents beside my plate. There was also a brown-paper parcel from Aunt Adelheide, postmarked New York City.

Since it was my birthday, we had scrambled eggs with our bread and preserves. Eggs were hard to get these days and were a real treat.

"I got them from Frau Ludwig," Mutter said. "Her sister lives in the country, near Magdeburg, and brought the Ludwigs a basket of eggs when she came to visit last weekend."

I savored every bite of them. After I'd finished eating, I reached for my birthday cards. There was one from Petra, one from our Pioneer leader, Frau Hoffmann, one from Herr and Frau Sterns, and one from the Korths upstairs.

Finally I opened the envelope that said "S. Lauchert, Alt Mittelheim," in Oma's handwriting in the upper-left corner. Inside was a birthday card with purple and yellow pansies on the front, and a folded letter. Oma had written:

Dear Heidi,

It's so hard for me to believe you're thirteen! I remember my thirteenth birthday, when I was growing up in Berlin. My parents and brothers and I had a picnic in the Tiergarten Park and we went to hear a military band in an outdoor pavilion. My parents gave me a bonnet with roses, which I had seen at Wertheim's Department Store and wanted desperately. Perhaps that was how my love of flowers began!

Fritz joins me in wishing you a happy birthday. He is busy with the harvest. I tell him to take it easy because of his heart, but you know how he is! He just growls and says he'll "not be treated like an old man."

Tell your father to save some vacation time and bring you all down here this fall. Your school is out for a week in October, isn't it? Come then! I'll just make your birthday cake late this year.

Lots of love, Oma

"She wants us to visit in October," I told Mutter and Vater. "Can we?"

"We'll see," Vater said.

"Aren't you going to open your presents?" Mutter asked.

From my parents I got a stylish short blue skirt, two oranges, a big chocolate bar, and the two latest issues of *Bravo* girls' magazine.

"Thank you!" I cried, and got up to hug them both. I knew they'd sneaked everything over from West Berlin, past the border police. You couldn't get any of those things here in the East.

I saved my present from Aunt Adelheide to open last. It was a pair of blue jeans, from New York! "Your mother told me your size," she'd written on the card. "I know how popular these are, and thought they might be hard to get in the East."

Hard to get? They were *impossible* to get in East Germany and were expensive in West Berlin. I unfolded them reverently and ran my fingers over the denim. I'd be the envy of every girl in my class. Even though our government didn't like us to wear clothes from Western countries, we did, anyway, when we could get them. They were a lot cuter than what we had in our stores.

"I'm going to try on the skirt and jeans," I told my parents.

The skirt fit perfectly. The jeans were a little long, but Mutter looked at the tag and said they were cotton and would shrink in the wash. I'd wear them to the zoo, I decided, then wear the skirt to dinner.

I felt like a fashion model as I walked to the Hansens' apartment house. I hoped that Petra or her mother would come to the door, but it was stout, blond-bearded Herr Hansen who opened it.

"Friendship!" he said with a curt nod. His eyes raked my blue jeans.

"Friendship," I replied. I seldom used that greeting, which stood for "Friendship with the Soviet

Union," but I didn't want to annoy Herr Hansen. He frightened me, with his piercing eyes and his gruff ways. Besides, I'd heard him call me "that border crosser's daughter." I knew what he thought: it wasn't proper for Petra, the daughter of an up-and-coming executive in the Ministry of the Interior, to be friends with the daughter of a border crosser.

"Come in, come in," he said impatiently, motioning for me to come inside.

"Hello, Heidi." Petra's mother came out of the kitchen. "Oh, look at your jeans!"

"They're from my aunt Adelheide," I said. "She's on vacation in America."

Petra admired practically every seam of my new pants. "You look like a teenager should. I wish *I* had an aunt Adelheide."

Herr Hansen said loudly, "In America, blue jeans are nothing special. They're just work clothes for laborers to wear."

There was an uncomfortable silence. I looked at the floor, wishing I could think of a good retort. Then Frau Hansen cleared her throat and said gently, "I think blue jeans are very popular with young people everywhere."

Herr Hansen sniffed, and brushed past me as he went into the living room.

"We need to get going," Petra said, sounding nervous. Even though she never said so, I often thought that she and her mother were scared of Herr Hansen, too.

After we got outside, I said, "Your father doesn't like me, does he?"

"Of course he does," she replied a little too quickly.

We walked to the Bernauer Strasse subway stop and bought tickets to the Zoo station. The subway car was crowded and stifling. At Alexanderplatz, we switched to an above-ground city train, which would take us the rest of the way. It crossed into the West at Friedrichstrasse and made three more stops before it pulled into the large, busy station.

"Where shall we go first?" Petra asked as we walked to the zoo entrance. "You get to choose, since it's your birthday."

Without any hesitation, I replied, "Let's visit Knautschke."

"I knew you'd say that!" Petra laughed. Knautschke the hippo was our favorite animal there.

As usual, the hippos were under water in their pool. We could see them through a special glass wall in the exhibit building.

"I think that's him," I said, pointing to the largest shadowy figure.

We watched the shapes of the hippos lumbering

around in the murky green water. Once a broad, dark snout came up for a noisy breath of air, but we weren't sure whether it belonged to Knautschke or his wife, Bulette. After a while, we went outside and over to a pile of large, flat rocks, where the two young hippos were eating whatever it was they got fed. The sign said the baby was named Jule, and her older sister was Jutte.

"I'm glad Jule isn't *our* new baby," I said. "She's as big as my bed."

Petra said, "I can see your mother shoving her into your room and saying, 'Heidi, meet your new sister!' "

Our laughter seemed to offend Jule, because she turned her tail toward us.

We left the hippos to watch the pelicans and the bears get fed. Then we visited the gorillas and went into fits of giggles deciding which ones looked like which of our teachers. Petra didn't want to go see the baboons because she became embarrassed by their pink bottoms, so we moved on to the giraffes, got ice cream bars, strolled around the lakes, and walked through the elephant house. We had a terrific time.

From the zoo we went to a sidewalk café for slices of fruit torte and a little pot of coffee. I seldom drank coffee and wasn't sure I liked the taste of it, but I felt grown-up and sophisticated as we sipped it and ate our torte. Petra gave me my birthday present, and watched as I tore off the pink wrapping paper and opened the small box.

Inside, on blue velvet, was a gold heart-shaped pendant on a delicate chain. "It's beautiful!" I cried. "Oh, Petra, I love it!"

She looked pleased and a little shy. "I got it at a shop over here."

"I know. There's nothing this pretty in *our* stores." I traced the heart with my finger. Petra must have saved her allowance for weeks to buy this. "I'm going to put it on right now."

"Let me fasten it for you."

She came over and fastened the gold chain around my neck.

"This has been a perfect day," I said. "I wish it never had to end."

"You still have dinner to look forward to," Petra reminded me. "Where did you decide to go?"

"The Radio Tower," I replied. "Vater said I can have all the Coca-Colas I want."

We took the subway back and hugged goodbye when we parted ways. I hummed a tune as I walked home from the station.

Vater decided it was too hot to wear his suit to the restaurant, but said that just for me he'd wear a nice shirt and his good trousers. Mutter wore a red flowered maternity top and a black skirt, and I helped her put her hair up in a French roll. I put on my new skirt and a white blouse that showed off the necklace Petra had given me. My parents both admired the little gold pendant.

"Petra has good taste," Vater mused, inspecting it closely. "She must be a very good friend."

I smiled. "She is."

Mutter said she felt like getting some exercise, so we walked to the Rosenthaler Platz subway station, which was a little farther than the Bernauer Strasse station. At Alexanderplatz we changed to a city train and rode a long way into West Berlin, several stops past the Zoo station. In spite of the ice cream and fruit torte I'd had with Petra, I was starving by the time we got to the Radio Tower.

For dinner I had a pork cutlet, potatoes, and cucumber salad. Mutter had smoked goose and potato dumplings, and Vater had a pig hock and sauerkraut. They had wine, and I had two Coca-Colas. For dessert, we all three had sherbet and fruit. My parents had coffee with theirs, and I had a third Coca-Cola. We lingered for a long time, watching the sky turn to turquoise, mauve, pink, and peach as the sun set.

We walked back to the station, enjoying the balmy evening breeze. Vater kept his arm around Mutter, and helped her over the rough places in the pavement. It was a long ride back home, and I nearly fell asleep as the city train made its way across Berlin. At Alexanderplatz, we changed to the subway and went northward to our neighborhood.

"Wake up, Heidi!" Vater said, shaking my arm. "We're at our stop."

"You and Petra must have walked a lot today," Mutter said as I followed her and Vater off the subway car. "Why don't you go to bed early tonight and—"

We all three stopped and stared in disbelief. There on the station platform was a huge sign. In heavy, black capital letters, it said:

**THESE PEOPLE ARE
BORDER CROSSERS
AND WARMONGERS!!**

Below that caption was a list of half a dozen names. One of them was Vater's.

4

THAT WAS ONLY THE START OF THE HARASSMENT. The next morning, while Mutter was still asleep, Vater and I were having breakfast when someone jabbed our door buzzer. *Bzzz-bzzz-bzzz!* it went, sounding like an angry bee. *Bzzz-bzzz-bzzz!*

"I'm coming," Vater grumbled, getting up.

I heard him open the door and say, "Good morning. Can I help you?"

"Friendship, Herr Klenk," a man said. Then, stiffly, as though he had memorized his lines and had to say them perfectly, he continued, "We are some of your neighbors, and we have come to say that we deplore your selfishness and lack of patriotism in continuing to work in West Berlin. Can't you see that it's unfair for you to deny your skills to East Germany when the government has provided you with a free education and gives your family free health care and low rent?"

"I bring valuable West German money into our economy," Vater replied. "That helps East Germany as much as my skills—"

"You're a warmonger!" another man broke in. "You support the Western countries, which are building bombs to drop on our ally the Soviet Union."

"You're a traitor to this country!" a woman cried. "People like you should be shot!"

I gasped. How dare they talk like that to my father?

Vater replied calmly, "I *was* shot, serving my country during the war. I still have the scars on my chest where they removed the bullet. Furthermore, I'm looking for a job here in the East. I've already had two offers, and I have interviews with three other employers. Is there anything else you wish to discuss?"

There was a short silence. Then the first man said, "Why—uh, no, it sounds as though everything is in order." He cleared his throat. "Good day, Herr Klenk."

Vater closed the door.

I ran over and hugged him. "You were wonderful, Vater! I just wish you didn't have to leave Herr Sterns's shop."

He returned my hug, and whispered, "So do I."

Later that morning, while he was at work and Mutter was visiting Frau Korth, our door buzzer sounded again. I started to open the door, then hesitated. What if it was another group of angry neighbors? I knew I couldn't handle them as well as Vater had.

"Heidi?" came a voice. "Frau Klenk? Are you there? It's me, Petra."

Relieved, I flung open the door. "Hi! I wasn't expecting you today. I'm glad you're here, though—I have tons of things to tell you. Go on back to my room while I get us some sodas. You can look at the new *Bravo*s I got for my birthday."

She came into the hallway, but then she just stood there, fiddling with her jacket ties and looking uncomfortable. "I can't stay," she said.

I blinked at her. "What's wrong?"

"Well—I just stopped by to tell you that my father saw a sign at the Bernauer Strasse subway station last night on his way home from work. It said—"

"I know. We saw it, too."

"Oh." Petra watched her hands twist and smooth the jacket ties. Then she looked at me, and all the words came out in a rush. "My father won't let me see you anymore! He says now that he's been promoted, he can't have people saying that his daughter is friends with a border crosser's daughter. It wouldn't look right."

I just stared at her, too stunned to say anything.

"I told him your father is looking for a job in the

East," she continued. "He said that once your father has found something over here, I can see you again."

"B-but until then . . . ?" I stammered.

"Until then I'll try to sneak over and visit you when he and my mother go out." She shrugged helplessly. "I don't know what else to do."

I felt sick. "I have to sit down. Come on into the living room."

We sat down on the couch and looked at our laps, not knowing what to say.

Finally Petra cleared her throat. "I do have one idea."

"What?"

She hesitated. "I was thinking that maybe if you tell your father about this, he'll try harder to find a job over here. I'm sure he can find something! After all, our government guarantees everybody a job. If he can't find an opening for a mechanic, he can work in a factory or something."

"I don't want him to work in a factory or something!" I cried. "He loves working on cars. Besides, it's bad enough that he has to leave Herr Sterns and that the neighbors are calling him a traitor. I'm not going to make him feel worse than he already does."

Petra was playing with her jacket ties again. "But, Heidi," she said slowly, "you have to admit that it's not fair for him to be working in the West for high wages when your family is getting the benefits provided by our government."

I knew Petra was repeating her father's words. Still, I was furious. "Petra, I can't believe you said that. You *know* my father isn't trying to get rich. He works at Sterns's because he's been there forever and he likes it there. And he's trying to find a job over here. He's even had two job offers already. He's just waiting for a better one."

"But don't you think it's unfair for him to be so particular about the job he takes? He *owes* it to East Germany to work over here and help build our perfect society. Besides, look at the problems he's causing you and your mother."

I jumped up, furious. "Look here, Petra Hansen, I'm proud of my father! He's doing the best he can, and I won't stand for you saying these things."

"Okay, okay!" She raised her hands, palms outward, in surrender. "Don't be angry. It's just that I promised Ulrike I'd talk to you about it, and——"

"You promised *Ulrike?*"

"Yes. You see——"

"All I see is that you'd better leave," I said coldly. "Now."

"But let me explain!"

"Just *leave.* Go tell your pal Ulrike that you kept your promise."

"All right," she said quietly, and got up. "I'm sorry I made such a mess of things."

After she had gone, I went to my room and scooped up the necklace she had given me from the top of my dressing table. It felt cool and fragile in my hand. I couldn't bring myself to throw it into the trash, so I tossed it toward the back of a wardrobe drawer and shoved a pile of socks over it. Then I curled up on my bed and held Max close.

"I can't believe she acted like that," I whispered to him. It wasn't Petra's fault that her father wouldn't let her see me. But for her to lecture me on Vater's responsibilities because *Ulrike* wanted her to! I could see the two of them, sitting in the Eisensteins' luxurious high-rise apartment. "I tried to talk to Heidi about her father," Petra would tell her new friend, "but she got mad and threw me out."

The next day, I ran errands, helped with the housework, and tried not to think about Petra. I didn't tell my parents about our fight, because I didn't want them to know what she had said about Vater. He'd feel terrible if he found out we had fought about him! When Mutter asked if I had any weekend plans with her, I said, "No, she's busy with a Pioneer project right now." Mutter gave me a quizzical look, but I pretended not to see it.

Vater had another interview Saturday morning,

at an auto shop in the Treptow District, south of us. When he got home, his face was sad and he sounded more discouraged than ever.

"The shop is short of mechanics, and the manager jumped at the chance to hire me," he said. "He seemed nice, and appeared to be doing the best he can—but the shop is run down and has almost no spare parts in stock."

"So you're not going to take the job?" I asked.

Vater sighed deeply and said, "I'll have to think about it."

I saw a meaningful look pass between him and Mutter. That night, the two of them stayed up and talked long after I'd gone to bed.

I remembered a game book I'd once had, where you drew lines to connect dots and make pictures. You had to connect a certain number of the dots before you could tell what the picture was going to be. Well, now I felt as if I were playing connect-the-dots again, trying to make a whole picture out of the whispered words and phrases I'd overheard. But this time it wasn't a game.

On Sunday, Vater and I were going to the garden to weed, water, and pick the vegetables that were ripe. When we opened our door to leave, there was a sign taped to it. Like the one on the subway platform, it was in heavy black type. It said:

HERE LIVES A TRAITOR!!!
By working in the West
and supporting the war lovers,
Herr Klenk has made himself our enemy!

Vater swore and savagely pulled it down. He ripped it in half and went to throw it into the kitchen trash can. I closed the door and followed him.

"What's wrong?" Mutter came out of the living room. "What is it?"

"Nothing," he replied shortly.

But Mutter saw the torn sign and stopped his hands before he could drop it in the trash. When she put the pieces together and read the words, she gave a little cry. "Karl Franz, I can't take this much longer!" she said, sobbing.

"You won't have to." Vater raised the lid of the trash can and stuffed in the sign. "I told you, Heinrich is—"

He looked at me as though he'd just remembered I was there. I wondered what he had been going to say about Herr Sterns, and why he'd stopped.

"Heidi, I need to stay here with your mother. Do you think you can go to the garden by yourself?"

"Yes, of course, Vater."

"All right. Go straight there and come home right afterward, understand?" He dug into his pocket.

"Here's some change for your tickets, and the keys to the garden gate and the cottage. You can keep them. I have a spare set."

I put the money into my coin purse, and slipped the keys onto the ring with my apartment key. Then I kissed Mutter goodbye, and held up the basket and pail. "I'll bring these back full, and I'll help you fix dinner."

She gave me a little smile, and Vater patted my shoulder as I left.

It was exciting to go across the city on my own, but I felt anxious about the garden. Someone might have found out that our garden belonged to a border crosser, and destroyed it! I pictured plants ripped up by the roots, vegetables smashed to a pulp, and marigold blooms torn from their stems. At my stop, I got off the train and ran all the way to the garden.

Everything was okay. I leaned against the cottage to catch my breath, then started to work. Gardening was so simple! If seedlings grew too close together, you thinned them; if weeds invaded the bean patch, you pulled them out; if plants looked dry, you watered them; if vegetables were ripe, you picked them. Why couldn't Vater's job situation be that easy? If you couldn't find a job you liked in East Berlin, you worked in West Berlin. Simple. But it *wasn't* simple, because if too many people worked in the West we'd never have our perfect society here in the East. On the other hand, it didn't seem right for Vater to have to work in a place with rats and a shortage of tools and spare parts.

As I knelt and pulled weeds, the quiet of the garden was broken by sirens wailing and horns tooting. I jumped up, my heart pounding, then realized that the people in nearby gardens were laughing and waving at the sky.

"What's happening?" I called to the family in the plot across the path from ours.

The daughter, who was a dark-haired girl, a little older than I was, replied, "The Soviet Union's cosmonaut, Titov, is orbiting the earth, and his spacecraft is overhead!"

"Where?" I asked, my eyes skimming the sky.

"You can't see it, but the officials know when it's scheduled to be over Berlin." She joined her family in waving wildly at the sky and crying, "Friendship, Herr Titov!"

I waved and yelled, too. I'd heard about Titov and his craft, *Vostok 2*, on the television news. It was actually going to orbit the earth many times, not just stay up in space for a short spell as the Americans' manned spacecraft had. I couldn't help feeling proud. The Soviet Union, our close friend and ally, was ahead in the space race! It was showing that a socialist country could beat the wealthier, more sophisticated Western countries.

After the sound of the sirens had faded out, the family and I gaily waved to one another, and went back to work. Before I left the garden, I filled the basket with carrots, spinach, tomatoes, broccoli, and two cabbages to take home. There weren't as many beans as there'd been last week, but I got enough for one meal.

Even with all the fresh vegetables, our supper that evening was unhappy. My parents were tired and on edge. They quibbled about little things, and Mutter scolded me for getting a green spinach stain on my place mat. I tried to cheer them up by telling them about *Vostok 2* going overhead, but Mutter just whispered, "Yes, the Soviets can put a man in space, but they can't put fresh food in the grocery stores," and Vater added, "What good does a spaceship do us when we don't have the tools to repair our cars?"

The next morning, after Vater had gone to work, Mutter and I were eating breakfast and watching the news about *Vostok 2*'s safe landing when there was a knock at the door.

"I'll get it," I said, pushing back my chair.

Mutter said, "If it's another group of neighbors, tell them your father will have a job in the East soon."

It wasn't a group of neighbors; it was our building

supervisor, Herr Brecht. Usually when he saw me he said merrily, "Hello, Fräulein Klenk!" Today his face was stern and there was no jolliness in his voice when he asked to speak with Mutter.

"Yes, just a moment," I said, but Mutter was already behind me.

"Go finish your breakfast," she said, patting me on the shoulder as she came to the door. "Good morning, Herr Brecht. What can I do for you?"

I sat down at the table again and began spreading margarine on a piece of bread. Over the drone of the television news, I heard our supervisor say briskly, "I'm sorry, Frau Klenk, but I can give your husband only two more weeks to get a job in the East. If he cannot bring me a certificate of employment by August twenty-first, your family will be evicted."

Evicted! I sat perfectly still, not breathing, the bread and knife in my hands.

Mutter said, "He has had several job offers, but he's hoping for a better one. Since many employers are on vacation right now, our town hall has given him until September tenth."

"I give him only until August twenty-first," Herr Brecht said firmly. "There are other people who want this apartment."

"But we've lived here for nearly fifteen years!" Mutter's voice was angry now. "We've always paid our rent on time, and we've never caused any trouble. Surely you'd rather have us than take a chance on new tenants."

"Tell your husband what I have said. Good day, Frau Klenk."

From the slam of the door and my mother's angry cry, I knew that Herr Brecht had walked away. I ran into the hallway.

Mutter was running her fingers through her hair. "Ugh, that horrid man! The nerve of him, wanting to throw us out after all these years—and me in this condition!"

"Why didn't you remind him of the baby?" I asked, although I didn't see how anyone who looked at Mutter could need to be reminded. "Surely he'd have said we could stay until after the baby's born!"

Mutter shook her head. "I wasn't going to beg, not after the way he acted. Hmmph! I'd rather have my baby in—in the *park* than grovel before that man."

I thought of Jule and her family, and began to giggle hysterically. Then my giggles turned into sobs, and when I told Mutter we'd be just like the hippo family at the zoo, bathing in a pool and eating off rocks, she couldn't understand what I was saying.

She handed me a tissue. "I'm sure your father will get a new job soon and we won't be evicted. I'm just angry because Herr Brecht talked to me like that. Now let's finish breakfast. We need to clean the apartment this morning."

I dried my eyes. "But we just cleaned it."

"I'm talking about a different kind of cleaning."

Over breakfast she explained. "Until your father gets a new job, we don't know what might happen," she said in a low voice. "Herr Brecht might insist on coming into the apartment, or send in a repairman to spy on us. Someone might even call the police with a made-up complaint about us. At any rate, we have to be prepared. That means we need to go through the apartment and gather up all our Western magazines and newspapers."

"We don't have to throw them out, do we?" I asked, thinking of my stack of *Bravo* magazines. Petra and I had spent hours poring over the beauty tips, advice columns, and articles on singers and movie stars.

Mutter shook her head. "We can't throw them out. Someone might see us putting them in the trash. We'll have to hide them."

After breakfast we turned our home into the Perfect East German Family's Apartment. We listened to rousing East German marches on the radio as we gathered up our West German magazines—Mutter's *Freundin* women's magazines, my *Bravo*s, and Vater's *Auto*s. We put them in a suitcase, spread clothes over them, and put the locked suitcase in my parents' wardrobe. Then we set all the TV and radio dials to East German stations.

"Always set them there after you've listened to a Western station," Mutter directed.

We pulled out some of the East German government leaflets that often turned up in our mailbox or outside our door, and scattered them around the apartment. We put a pile of them on the coffee table. I added a booklet I'd been given in the Pioneers called *The Future Is Ours*, with poems about East Germany and inspiring stories of brave and honorable citizens. The cover showed East German soldiers and factory workers, a girl helping bring in the wheat harvest, a boy waving an East German flag, and a farmer in a green tractor like the ones on Opa Fritz's cooperative.

"Mutter," I said, "if we *were* to be evicted, would we go to Opa Fritz's?"

She didn't answer for a moment, and I wished I hadn't asked. The idea that we could always go live at the farm had been a comfort to me. I didn't want it to be taken away.

Mutter said, "We won't be evicted, Heidi. I told you." Then she straightened a row of government pamphlets on the shelf where her *Freundin*s had been, and added, "I suppose Opa Fritz would let us stay at the farm in an emergency. We couldn't live there for long, though. It wouldn't be fair to him and Oma. Besides, if the problem involved your father's job, I don't know how sympathetic Opa Fritz would be."

I nodded. I guessed that, deep down, I'd known that living at the farm wouldn't work. Opa Fritz and Vater could talk with each other for hours about mechanical parts and repair techniques. But when the talk turned to politics, we knew there'd be trouble. Opa Fritz liked the socialist farming system, in which the government took control of all the farms in an area, combined them into one huge cooperative, and gave the farmers wages, bad-crop insurance, and old-age pensions in return for their crops. Vater thought it was terrible for the government to take over a farmer's property and leave him with only his house, a garden, and a few animals to call his own. I knew that Opa Fritz wouldn't be very sympathetic if we got evicted because of Vater's working in the West.

When we'd finished cleaning, Mutter stood in the doorway and looked at the living room. She nodded in satisfaction. "Nobody can find anything to criticize here."

Nobody except me, I thought. Our home didn't look like *home* anymore.

That night I had my nightmare again. I was swimming in a sparkling blue lake under a sunny sky, but suddenly everything turned dark and terrifying. I churned my arms and legs frantically, but I couldn't move. The evil black water closed in over my head and filled my mouth and nose. No matter how hard I tried to pull myself up into the air above, something held me down. I kicked and flailed desperately, but I couldn't get away.

When I woke up, I lay staring at the ceiling, my heart pounding. It was too hot to go back to sleep, so I decided to get some orange soda from the refrigerator.

But there was a dim light coming from the kitchen, and when I got closer, I could hear my parents whispering. It was three in the morning, and they were still whispering!

Suddenly I was certain of something: I'd had enough of these secret sessions that didn't include me. I was tired of trying to connect the dots.

Tomorrow, I thought, I'm going to tell them that I want to know what they're talking about. Even if I'm not a grown-up, I'm a member of this family, and I have a right to know.

5

THE NEXT MORNING, I DECIDED I would wait and talk to my parents at supper, when we would all be together and no one would have to rush off anywhere.

But to my amazement, after I'd wished my parents good morning, Vater said, "Heidi, your mother and I need to talk to you after breakfast."

"Aren't you going to work this morning?" I asked.

"Yes, but not for a while yet. Heinrich will understand if I'm late."

I knew by the serious tone of his voice that I wouldn't have to ask what the whispers had been about. He and Mutter were going to tell me.

I fixed a bowl of cereal and a cup of tea, and took them to the table. We ate silently. Mutter took our dishes to the kitchen, then poured Vater and herself more coffee.

In a low voice, Vater said, "What we're going to tell you is very important, and you must listen carefully. You also cannot tell anyone—or even hint to anyone—the subject of this conversation. If anyone finds out what we're going to do, we'll be sent to prison. Understand?"

I nodded.

He rested his forearms on the table and leaned close to me. Slowly he said, "The first part is good news. Heinrich Sterns has decided to retire soon, and he wants me to become a partner in the shop. When he retires, I'll become the new owner."

I shook my head, confused. "But how can you, when you have to get a job in East Berlin?"

"That's the second part of what I have to tell you. Heinrich's offer helped your mother and me decide on something we'd already discussed." He paused, then whispered, "Heidi, the three of us are going to move to West Berlin."

I stared at him, disbelieving. "Move? You mean, *defect*? Leave everything behind?"

"That's what I mean. We have it all planned. Heinrich Sterns has found us an apartment, in the Wedding District, just around the corner from where my co-worker Hans Bauer and his wife live."

"So we won't have to go to the refugee center," Mutter put in.

Refugee. I'm going to be a refugee, I thought dazedly.

I whispered, "But my whole life is in the East!"

"I know that." Vater grimaced. "We know that this will be hard for you, but we think it's necessary. Like I said, we were thinking about leaving here even before Heinrich made the offer. It's not just because of my job situation. What's even more important is that over here we'll never have a say in the way things are done. The government will continue to run our lives. Herr Ulbricht and the others will dictate where we work, what TV stations we can watch, what books we can read, and where we're allowed to travel. We'll always have to be careful what we say and do, and worry about people spying on us. Someday we might even be forced to spy on our friends. We don't want to keep living like this, and we don't want you and your little brother or sister to live like this."

Mutter said, "We're afraid that if we don't leave soon, we'll never get out. Many people are saying that our leaders are going to close the border with West Berlin."

I blinked at her. "What do you mean, close it? How could they?"

"They could put up a barbed wire fence and station guards along it," Mutter replied, "just like the border that separates East Germany and West Germany. Some people say the government could even build a wall between the two parts of Berlin."

I remembered something. "Herr Ulbricht said no one is planning to put up a wall. He said that just a couple of months ago. My teachers talked about it."

Mutter said, "I know, but people are asking *why* he said that. Nobody had ever mentioned a wall until then—so why did he suddenly start talking about it, unless the government was thinking of building one? Besides, there are rumors that Herr Ulbricht has sneaked off to Moscow to meet with his boss, Premier Khrushchev of the Soviet Union. And last night on television, Khrushchev gave a speech. We saw part of it on the news while you were listening to the radio. Among other things, he told Westerners, 'Your loophole into East Germany will soon be closed.'"

"President Kennedy of the United States also made a speech recently," Vater added. "He promised to protect *West* Berlin, but he didn't say anything about us. The United States and the Soviet Union are both building up their military forces, too."

"Do you think there will be a war?" I asked.

"Nobody knows," Vater said. "But things are coming to a head, and we expect that the border will be closed soon. Once it's closed, there will be no more trips over to West Berlin to work or shop, and no chance to escape from the Eastern Sector. We'll be trapped here for the rest of our lives."

"But when we've built our ideal society—"

"That ideal society's a myth!" Vater whispered fiercely. "I know what you've learned in school and in the Pioneers, but that ideal society our leaders talk about is never going to exist. If we don't get out soon, we could be stuck here forever with exactly the same conditions we have now."

I swallowed hard. "When will we go?"

Vater replied, "This Saturday."

"This *Sat*urday!" I cried. "That's—that's four days from now."

Everything was spinning in my head, making me feel dizzy. We were going to leave in four days. For good. We would never come back. We couldn't come back, even to visit, because if anybody recognized us and called the police, we'd be thrown into prison for *Republikflucht*—fleeing the Republic of East Germany.

"We had planned to wait until after the baby was born," Mutter explained, "but then last week Herr Sterns found us the apartment and we had to decide whether or not to take it. Also," she added, glancing at Vater, "something happened a couple of weeks ago that has made us want to go as soon as possible."

"What was it?" I asked.

Mutter took a deep breath. "A pregnant East Berlin woman whose husband was a border crosser went to the local hospital because she was having a miscarriage. When the hospital staff found out her husband worked in West Berlin, they refused to admit her. They told her she had no right to get free medical care over here when her husband was earning a high salary in the West. Her husband rushed her across to a hospital in West Berlin, but by the time they got there, she had lost too much blood. She died soon after they arrived."

"It could have been you!" I whispered, horrified. Those people would have let my mother and my new brother or sister *die* just because Vater worked in the West! I didn't want to believe it, but I remembered the sign on our door and Herr Brecht's threats and the neighbor who had said that Vater should be shot, and I knew that it was true.

Mutter said, "It could still *be* me if the baby comes while we live over here and anything goes wrong. Emmy Bauer is also expecting and has recommended a good doctor in the West. I have an appointment with him tomorrow."

Vater cleared his throat. "Let's talk about what we'll do on Saturday. Your mother and I will go West together on the subway. She'll have an overnight bag and pretend to be in labor. If the border police stop us, I'll explain that my job in the East hasn't started yet and that I'm taking her to a West Berlin hospital to be certain she gets admitted. After the outcry in the West over that woman who died, I don't think they will dare detain us." He paused. "You'll come over on the same day, but on another train. Just dress normally and pretend you're going shopping or to a movie."

"Don't I get to take an overnight bag, too?"

Vater shook his head. "It will be safer if you don't."

"You mean I can't take anything?"

"No, but we've thought of some ways to send a few things over beforehand. And I do mean a *few*. You'll have to think hard about what you want to send."

"What's our new apartment like?" I asked. I needed to be able to picture myself in the new life I was going to have.

Vater said, "It's in an old building that survived the war. It's ugly on the outside, but it's on a quiet street, and the apartments are large. Ours has a living room, two bedrooms, a kitchen, and a lavatory. There's no bathtub—we'll have to use a central bathroom down the hall, or get a portable tub and bathe in the kitchen. The Sternses and Bauers are lending us linens and dishes, and I've bought a sofa, table, and beds. Heinrich has given me some time off to get the apartment ready."

"Where will I go to school?"

"I'm not sure, Heidi. We'll look into that once we're there."

"The important thing is that we'll be together and safe and free," Mutter said gently. "We can deal with everything else."

I nodded, but I felt as if I were being asked to close my eyes and jump off a cliff. I couldn't imagine leaving everything—my home, my school, my friends. Petra! I thought suddenly. What would I do about Petra? I was still angry at her, but I didn't want never to see her again.

Vater said, "Before we go, we must do all we can to hide our preparations and keep people from knowing we're planning to leave. Tomorrow I'll go to the auto shop in Treptow and accept the job the manager offered. I'll say that I'll start work on September first, after my two-week vacation from Sterns's is over."

"We've also bought some baby furniture from the Korths," Mutter added. "We'll have to leave it behind, but we want the neighbors to think we're planning to stay here. You can help, too: sign up for some Pioneer activities, make plans with Petra, talk about the fall school term. Tell people that your father has found a job here in the East, and that we're very happy and relieved."

Vater said, "You need to decide now, this morning,

what you want to take with you. Don't make a list or put things in a pile, though. We don't want anything in the apartment to look out of the ordinary."

As I got up to go to my room, Vater stopped me. "One more thing. We know you and Petra are close friends. But you cannot tell her about this, or say anything that might make her suspect we're preparing to leave. Her father is loyal to the government, and if she said anything that made him suspicious, he would turn us in without a second thought. Understand?"

"Yes, Vater." Slowly I added, "Actually, Petra and I sort of had a fight and I won't be seeing her any time soon. I guess now that we're leaving on Saturday, I might never see her again."

"Oh, but you and Petra have been good friends for so long!" Mutter cried. "Surely you can make up with her before you go. Why don't you go see her tomorrow?"

"I'll think about it," I murmured. I didn't know whether I wanted to see her or not. Would she be the old Petra, or the Petra who had visited me on Thursday?

I went to my room and made a mental list of what to take. Max, for sure. My new blue skirt and jeans. What about my radio? I would miss it, but I didn't know whether there'd be room to take it. Besides, I could get another radio in the West—maybe a little transistor one with an earpiece, so I could listen to rock and roll without the neighbors hearing.

But in the West it wouldn't matter if the neighbors heard! I'd be able to listen to music openly. And I'd be able to travel, to see the places that Aunt Adelheide went. I decided that I should think about those things—what I would gain, instead of what I was leaving.

Still, it was unbelievable that after Saturday I'd never again see my room or hear the Weppelmanns or put on my red Pioneer scarf. I'd never again go to my school or our garden or the bakery and milk shop.

When the clock in the living room struck ten, I wondered whether we'd be able to take it West. If not, I'd miss hearing it say our names. "Karl Franz!" it said now. "Anne-marie! Hei-di! Frie-drich! So-phie!"

Suddenly I stopped, my hand on a blouse that hung in the closet. Once we'd moved to West Berlin, we'd never be able to go *anywhere in East Germany* again.

"The farm!" I cried.

I ran into the kitchen. My mother was drying and putting away the breakfast dishes.

"Mutter, we won't be able to go to the farm anymore!"

"Lower your voice," she whispered sternly. She set down the bowl she'd been drying and turned to face me. "Yes, I know that. Heidi, this decision was very hard on your father. Oma's his mother, and he knew that moving West would mean having to leave her. But he had to think about our future, about you and the baby."

I felt hot tears sliding down my face.

Mutter said, "Oma and I talked about this last summer when we were having breakfast together in her kitchen. You were still asleep, and the men were out in the barn. Even back then, your father and I were considering going West if things got worse here. I told Oma, and she urged us to go. She even said that if it weren't for Opa Fritz, she'd go with us. She said she was getting tired of all the cooperative's rules and the way the government demanded more and more of the crop every year. Besides, she's always loved going to church, and you know our government doesn't approve of that."

I sniffled, and Mutter handed me a handkerchief from her pocket.

"She specifically mentioned you, Heidi. She said that as much as she'd miss you, she hoped you would move West someday. She said, 'Heidi's a smart girl and I want her to be free to ask questions and make up her own mind about things—not just accept what she's told. I want her to see the world, too, like Adelheide.' "

"Oma said that?"

"Yes." Mutter hesitated. "Oma knows that she's

near the end of her life and you're near the beginning of yours. She wants what's best for you."

"But I can't stand to think I'll never see her and Opa Fritz again!"

"Then don't think it. After all, it might not turn out that way. If the border isn't closed immediately, Oma and Opa Fritz will be able to visit us as soon as the harvest is in. Besides, we'll be able to write back and forth, and send packages and photos. We won't completely lose touch." Mutter squeezed my shoulders. "I know it's very hard for you. I wish I could make it easier."

I hugged her and began crying again.

She said gently, " Let's go look through your clothes, and I'll help you choose what to take. We can pretend we're rearranging things to make room for the baby, in case the Weppelmanns can hear us."

Mutter was brisk and businesslike, which made it easier for me not to think about Oma and Opa Fritz or about Petra.

We looked through my wardrobe and drawers and decided what to send West. Every once in a while Mutter would say loudly, "Now, the baby's clothes can go in these drawers," or "I think the crib will fit in that corner," in case the creepy Weppelmanns were listening. We'd laugh sometimes, as though we were having a lot of fun getting ready for my new brother or sister.

Vater hadn't been exaggerating when he'd said I could take only a few things. I would wear my green cotton skirt and my striped blouse when I went West. But I could send just my new blue skirt, my jeans, two pairs of shorts, two shirts, a sweater, and some under-clothes.

"There's probably room for your swimsuit, too," Mutter said.

I shook my head. "No, I'll leave it. It doesn't fit anymore."

Actually, it had fit fine when I'd worn it to the Müggelsee in June, and I didn't think I had grown since then. But I knew I'd never swim again, so why take it?

I put aside a few other things to send: my birthday card from Oma, my postcards from Aunt Adelheide, and, although I wasn't sure why I wanted them, my Pioneer scarf and my booklet called *The Future Is Ours* with the poems and stories about East Germany. From my jewelry case I added a bead necklace I liked, a gold pin that my parents had given me for my tenth birth-day, and the tortoiseshell hair clip I sometimes wore when I dressed up.

Mutter said, "What about that pretty necklace Petra gave you for your birthday?"

I shrugged.

"Come here a minute. Let's talk." Mutter sat down on the bed and patted the place beside her.

I sat down, but I didn't look at her.

"You said earlier that you and Petra had a fight. Was it so serious that you don't even want to keep the necklace?"

Suddenly I couldn't keep my feelings to myself any longer. "Yes!" I whispered. "It was that serious. She told me it was unfair for Vater to work in the West. She made it sound like he was just trying to get rich."

Mutter sighed. "Sweetheart, she hears that kind of talk at home. You know what her father is like. I imagine poor Petra gets confused about what to believe."

"But she's also made friends with Ulrike Eisenstein." I said her name with distaste, as though I were saying "pimples" or "dirty laundry."

"Ulrike Eisenstein." Mutter considered. "Isn't she the girl with the long, pretty hair? The one who's on your Friendship Council?"

I nodded, making a face. "She's bossy and stuck up. I hate her! It was her, not Herr Hansen, who made Petra talk to me about Vater."

"If Ulrike's so important in the Pioneers, Petra can hardly refuse to do what she says," Mutter replied. "Don't you think you should go talk to Petra? She might want to tell you she's sorry."

I scowled at the floor. I didn't want to go to Petra's. What if I got there and she and Ulrike were lounging on the Hansens' sofa, drinking orange sodas and watching television, the way she and I used to do?

"Oh, honey, don't stay angry at her!" Mutter said. "This may be the last chance you ever have to make up with her. If you don't do it, you'll be sorry someday."

"Maybe I'll talk to her," I mumbled reluctantly. "I suppose I'll take the necklace."

I got up and found the little gold heart and chain underneath my socks. Mutter nodded her approval.

"How are we going to take Max?" I asked, to change the subject.

Mutter looked him over, considering. "Leave him out for now and we'll see."

"I'm not going to leave him here!" I whispered quickly.

"I know, honey. But we may need him to pad something or fill a space in a box."

That seemed disrespectful to Max, and I patted him on the head when my mother wasn't looking.

While we sorted clothes, I whispered, "Mutter, how can we walk away from our whole lives like this?"

"Hundreds of thousands of other people have done it," she whispered back. "Besides, think of all the people who lost their homes in the war when Berlin was bombed."

I thought about them, but not in the way Mutter had intended. What I thought was that if you had to lose your home, it *should* happen with bombs exploding, flames leaping, sirens wailing, people screaming, and the earth shaking under your feet. It shouldn't happen on just an ordinary day when nobody around you even knew that you were suffering.

Mutter added, "We'll have your father's income, an apartment to move into, and friends in the West. Most people who leave here have to go to a refugee shelter. We're very lucky."

I whispered, "I guess so." But I didn't feel lucky. I felt scared and sad, and I was already homesick.

6

THE FOLLOWING MORNING after Vater had gone to work, Mutter got ready for her doctor's appointment. "While I'm away," she asked, "would you do the shopping, please? First get bread and milk. Be sure to get the milk last—"

"So it doesn't spoil before I get home," I finished for her.

She laughed. "Yes, and then go to the big grocery store for canned goods. When you're there, you must forget that we'll be leaving in three days—just buy what you normally would. Also, try to get some little pastries if you can. Hans and Emmy Bauer will be visiting us this evening."

"They're the ones who'll be our new neighbors, aren't they?"

"Yes. We're having a party to celebrate that Emmy

and I are both expecting." She kissed the top of my head. "I'll be home as soon as I can. The Korths will be bringing down some baby furniture early this afternoon. Bye, sweetheart."

After she left, I felt uneasy. I wasn't used to being alone in the apartment, and it was spooky. Vater and Mutter would both be in the West. What if the border did get closed, right now, this morning, and I was stranded here while they were over there?

"How silly!" I whispered to Max as I made my bed. The border couldn't be sealed off *that* suddenly! Still, I felt nervous.

If Petra and I were still friends, I would stop by her apartment and ask her to go shopping with me. We'd stroll down the street gossiping and giggling, and I'd soon forget my fears. But Petra and I *weren't* friends anymore.

I turned on the television for company and watched the news on the East Berlin channel as I ate breakfast. Moscow was preparing for a huge parade that afternoon to honor Major Titov, who had spent more than twenty-four hours orbiting the earth. "Already the roads leading to Moscow are lined with cheering crowds," the newscaster said. "Tonight, at a ceremony at the Kremlin, Premier Khrushchev will award Major Titov the Order of Hero of the Soviet Union."

She added, "The glorious victory of Major Titov and his spacecraft, *Vostok 2*, far outshines anything the Western world has done."

The Western world. That was where I'd be living in a few days. Was it true what my teachers said: That the West was full of crime and rioting? That Westerners wanted to start a war with the Soviet Union and its allies? That most people over there cared only about making money?

I wondered what my new schoolmates would be like. Maybe they'd make fun of me. After all, I'd be not only a new girl but a refugee, less well dressed and less sophisticated. They'd probably expect me to tell them how much I hated the East, or to laugh at the jokes they made about it. If they did, I'd say, "I'm proud to be from East Germany! Things aren't perfect there, but the people work hard for peace and prosperity. Besides, how would *you* like to have to leave your home and your grandparents?"

The clock struck ten-thirty. I turned off the TV set, got the milk jug and shopping basket from the kitchen, and set off for the shops. The bakery had sold out of pastries and everything else except bread, so I got a loaf of that and the milk. I had just started home when I heard someone cry, "Eggs! They have eggs!"

I ran over to the shop where I'd heard the woman

shouting and got in line. Even if the milk spoiled, I felt sure Mutter would want me to try to get eggs. When I reached the counter, there were only two left and a long queue of people behind me. I hesitated, feeling guilty: after all, we'd be going West in two days and could have as many eggs as we wanted. But Mutter had said to shop as though we weren't preparing to leave.

"I'll take both," I said, handing my money to the woman behind the counter. As I left, the other people in line just shrugged or sighed in resignation.

I took home the eggs, milk, and bread and stored them in the kitchen. Then I caught the subway for the government-run grocery store. As usual, it had little to choose from: no meat or fresh produce, just neatly displayed cans, jars, and bottles. I put two cans of soup, a jar of beets, a can of goulash, and a jar of pickles in my basket.

As I went up to pay, the clerk beckoned to me. "Hurry along, Fräulein, you're the last customer. We're closing now."

"But it's only noon!"

She sniffed. "You can blame those filthy traitors who've fled West. They've left us with too few workers to keep the stores open in the afternoons."

I'd barely gotten out the door before she locked it. The metal shades rattled down over the windows, sounding angry, as though they knew that I, too, would soon be a filthy traitor who had fled West.

On my way back to the subway station, I passed a row of brightly colored banners proclaiming SOCIALISM WILL TRIUMPH! Considering the emptiness of the store, the words seemed mocking.

The uneasiness I had felt earlier settled over me again. Fear seemed to be in the East Berlin air, along with the suffocating heat and the drizzle. Everyone in the subway car sat silently, clutching their bags tightly and keeping their faces expressionless. Once in a while, we'd study each other surreptitiously, then quickly turn our eyes back down to our laps.

We're all scared, I thought. The people who are planning to leave are scared they'll be caught, and the people who are planning to stay are scared they'll be trapped. And all of us are sad and anxious because, whether we leave or stay, there will be people we love on the other side.

At the Weinmeisterstrasse stop, two East German policemen boarded the subway car and sat down in the seats across from me. As they talked to each other in low tones, they kept glancing at me. I began to tremble. Maybe they could read my mind and guess the secret it held. Or maybe there was something about me, something that only policemen could see, that said, "This girl is going to flee West!"

They aren't after me, I told myself. They're just riding the subway home, like the rest of us.

Still, as soon as we reached the next station, which was the stop before mine, I jumped up and got off the train. When it left with the policemen on it, I took a few deep breaths and tried to stop shaking. I'd walk the rest of the way home, I decided. It was only a few extra blocks, and maybe I'd feel less nervous if I was outside.

Halfway up Brunnenstrasse, I groaned, wishing I had stayed on the subway. Petra and Ulrike were sauntering down the sidewalk toward me, swinging their gym bags. It was too late for me to hide.

"Hi," Petra mumbled as we met. She looked down, studying the sidewalk.

"Hello, Heidi," Ulrike said. "Been shopping?"

"Yes," I replied. For the first time, I noticed how Ulrike smiled: her mouth turned up, but her eyes stayed cool and impassive, as though they belonged in another face. "Where have you been, to the pool?"

She nodded. "I'm teaching Petra how to dive. My coach said just last week that I could be a champion diver if I weren't so busy with schoolwork and running the Pioneers."

"That's nice," I said. "By the way, I have good news. My father has found a new job! He won't have to go over to the West anymore."

"That *is* good news," Ulrike said, smiling her mouth smile.

Petra looked up in surprise. "Did he find a job as a mechanic?"

"Of course he did," I said coolly. I turned back to Ulrike. "Well, I'd better be going. My parents are having some baby furniture delivered. I don't want them to move my bed out and give my whole room to the baby while I'm gone!"

We laughed and said goodbye. Ulrike walked on, but Petra put her hand on my arm.

"Come over tomorrow," she whispered.

"Why, so you can lecture me again?" Seeing her with Ulrike had rekindled all my anger. I shook her hand off and walked away.

Maybe, I thought, in a few days she would decide to come visit me. She would figure that since Vater now had a job in the East, I'd be willing to forget the things she'd said and be friends again. But imagine her shock when she walked down the hall to our apartment and was greeted by a big, blood-red seal on our door! That was what the police put on people's doors when they fled West. Petra would stare, not believing it. Then she'd turn and run away, sobbing. Perhaps she would realize that it had been people like *her* who had pressured my family into leaving.

I smiled, picturing her shocked face when she saw that seal. But then other Petra faces flashed through my mind: pink with sun and laughter as we watched the hippos at the zoo, shyly pleased as I thanked her for my birthday necklace, contorted in funny ways to cheer me up during boring classes, giggling as we lay on my bed and read the latest *Bravo*, and pale and wide-eyed with concern as she sat with me after my Müggelsee accident.

Suddenly the image of Petra standing there, stunned and crying, in front of that red seal no longer pleased me. Perhaps I *would* visit her tomorrow. Mutter was right: we'd been good friends for a long time. I shouldn't move away without making up with her. But she'd said those things about Vater because she'd promised *Ulrike* she would! That still made me feel hurt and angry.

I sighed. I'd think it over, and decide in the morning whether to go visit her.

Mutter got home soon after I did. She was thrilled with the two eggs I'd gotten.

"Now we'll be able to make a cake for the Bauers," she said. "We can use Oma's jam for filling, and we have enough margarine and sugar to make icing."

Right after lunch, Herr and Frau Korth made several trips downstairs to deliver the baby furniture. I had wondered why the Korths, who were nearly as old as Oma and Opa Fritz, had baby furniture, but Mutter explained that she and Vater had bought it from the Korths' son and daughter-in-law. I held open our door as they squeezed past with first a high chair, then a playpen, and finally a crib.

Frau Ludwig came over to see what was happening, and Herr Brecht arrived in time to help guide the crib down the steps. It occurred to me that the Weppelmanns were probably watching through the peephole in their door.

"Since you're buying furniture, I assume that your husband has found a job in the East," Herr Brecht said to Mutter after the crib was in our living room.

She replied happily, "Yes, at an auto shop down in the Treptow District. He'll start on the first of September."

Herr Brecht became his old jolly self again. "Excellent, Frau Klenk! I'm glad I won't have to lose you as tenants. Tell Herr Klenk to bring me a certificate of work from his new employer as soon as possible, and everything will be back to normal."

He winked jovially at me. I tried to smile in return, but I couldn't forget that he'd threatened to evict us.

After everyone had left, Mutter and I had lunch. The telephone rang as we were clearing the table, but when I answered it, nobody was there.

"This phone system!" Mutter rolled her eyes. "It's one thing I won't miss."

She got out her favorite recipe book, and I gathered the ingredients for the cake as she read them to me.

Since there was so little space in the kitchen, I put everything on the dining table and we worked there. Mutter whisked the egg yolks, and I lined the cake tin with paper.

I whispered, "Mutter, what do you think it will be like, living in the West?"

She considered. "We won't have to whisper, for one thing. Over there, people can say what's on their minds. We won't have to wait in line to buy eggs, either. I'll be able to plan meals, and if the baby needs special food, I'll be able to get it."

As she added the sugar to the yolks, she asked, "What do you think it will be like?"

I shrugged. "I don't know. I like the *idea* of being able to say what's on my mind, but I'm not sure I'll ever feel safe doing it. Besides, when I go over there, I feel addled, like my brain can't keep up. The cars move too fast, and there are too many colors and bright lights, and too many choices in the stores. You could go *crazy* trying to choose what movie to see or what flavor ice cream to ask for. Besides, what about all the crime over there? Aren't you scared we'll get robbed or beaten up? And there's the polio epidemic. I don't want to get polio."

"You won't, sweetheart. That epidemic isn't real.

Our government wants us to think it is so we'll be scared to go over there."

"But what if there's a war? We'd be dropping bombs on our friends here—on Oma and Opa Fritz!"

"We'll have to hope there isn't a war."

"But—"

Mutter turned to face me. "Heidi, we're going West. That's final. I can't promise that our lives over there will be easy. But we're going, so you may as well stop fretting."

"Yes, Mutter." Then I blurted out, "But how can we just stand here and make a cake when our lives are about to change so much?"

"It's all part of the plan," she whispered. "When Hans and Emmy Bauer come tonight, we'll be doing more than having a party. We'll also be giving them our clothes, papers, and money to sneak over the border for us."

"How will they do it without getting caught?" I asked.

"You'll see. They've thought up a clever plan."

Later that afternoon, while the cake was cooling, she said, "I need you to help me wrap a present."

"Is it for the Bauers?"

"It's for their baby," Mutter answered. She thought a moment. "Well, actually it's for *us*."

I collected tape, scissors, wrapping paper, and ribbon, while she found a large box. We put everything on my parents' bed.

"Now go get the clock from the living room," Mutter said.

"The *clock*?" I was puzzled. Then I thought about what she'd just said: the present was actually for us. Suddenly everything made sense. "I know! We're sending our things over to the West, wrapped up as a baby gift."

"That's right." Mutter nodded. "Some of them, anyway. Emmy has thought of another way to get our clothes over. And Max they can simply carry, like another baby gift."

By the time Vater got home, the cake was iced and the box was wrapped in pink-and-yellow paper with a white bow on top.

He looked tired and sad. "I stopped by the shop in Treptow to tell Herr Voss, the manager, that I had decided to accept the job he offered me. He was so pleased and grateful. I feel bad about being dishonest with him."

Mutter didn't reply. She just gave him a hug and a kiss.

I dressed in the green skirt and striped blouse I planned to wear West, and my parents put on the nice clothes they'd worn to dinner on my birthday. Vater moved the playpen and high chair into his and Mutter's room, and put the crib in its new place in my bedroom.

"There's hardly space to walk!" I said in dismay. Then I remembered that it didn't matter, since we would be leaving in a few days.

The Bauers arrived at seven-thirty. Hans was younger than Vater, with short blond hair, gray eyes, and rosy cheeks. He was wearing a gray suit with a blue tie.

Emmy had short, dark curls, brown eyes, a wide smile, and freckles across her nose. She was beautiful in her cream-colored maternity blouse and black skirt. I liked her immediately.

"Heidi, I'm glad to meet you," she said, hugging me. Then she and Mutter hugged, and laughed because they both stuck out so far they could hardly reach each other.

"Let's take some photos outside before it gets dark," Vater suggested, and got his camera. At first I didn't see why we needed to take the photos outside. But the adults talked and laughed so much as we went downstairs that I decided it must be so we could convince the neighbors that we were having a party. They could hardly suspect us of planning to defect when we were acting so happy and carefree.

Vater took photos outside our building of Mutter and Emmy standing together, of the two of them and me, and of Hans and Emmy. Then Hans took a photo of my parents and me. Finally we went back upstairs to have the cake and some of the Western coffee that the Bauers had brought as a gift.

As Vater was unlocking the door, we heard the telephone ringing. He rushed to answer it, but was too late. "I don't know who it was," he said, putting the receiver back on the set.

"Someone tried to call this afternoon, too," Mutter said. "Heidi, would you bring out the plates?"

My parents praised the coffee the Bauers had brought, and the Bauers praised the cake we had made. In case the neighbors could hear them, Mutter told Emmy that she was going to have her baby at the nearby hospital here in East Berlin. Then Vater told Hans, "The garage where I'll be working is a fine place. It's not as fancy as Herr Sterns's shop, but I don't care. I'm glad to have a job over here."

After we'd finished our cake and coffee, Mutter pushed back her chair and stood up. "Emmy, come back to the bedroom. Heidi and I will show you the new baby furniture."

When we got to my parents' room, Emmy admired the high chair and playpen. Mutter cupped her mouth up close to my ear.

"You'll be surprised at what happens next," she whispered. "But don't say anything the neighbors might overhear. You see, Emmy's really only three months pregnant."

"But she's as big as you are!"

Mutter continued, "It's mostly a cushion. Now go get the clothes you're sending."

When I got back to the bedroom with my little stack of clothes, Emmy had taken off her maternity top and was unwinding a wide elastic bandage from around her middle. She handed it to Mutter along with the small cushion it had bound to her midsection. Now she was nearly as slender as I was. Mutter took the pillowcase off the cushion and put in the clothes she and I were sending West.

As Emmy held the new "baby" in place on her belly, Mutter wrapped the bandage around it and secured the end.

"What about Vater's clothes?" I asked.

"He's already taken them West," Mutter whispered. "He took extra work clothes and left them at the shop on several days. He told the border police he needed them since he gets so dirty at work. Once he wore his suit over there and left it, and wore work clothes home. He's also been wearing extra underclothes and socks, and leaving them at the shop."

When we went back out to the living room, Emmy

looked just as she had when she'd arrived. I saw Mutter give Vater and Hans a little nod.

The adults had some more coffee, and Hans ate the last piece of cake. Just before the Bauers left, Mutter gave them the gift we'd wrapped.

"Go get Max," she told me.

When I picked him up from the bed, I kissed him and whispered, "See you on Saturday."

To my great embarrassment, tears ran down my face as I handed him to Emmy. She whispered, "He's darling! I'll take good care of him, Heidi. And don't worry. You'll like it in the West. We live in the same neighborhood you're moving to, and I'll introduce you to some nice kids there."

"Thanks," I said gratefully.

We walked with the Bauers to their car. Hans carefully put the box in the trunk, and Emma put Max beside it. I waved goodbye to him when nobody was looking.

"Come back and bring the baby!" Mutter told the Bauers, and Emmy said, "You come visit us and bring yours, too." Vater told Hans to say hello to everyone at the shop.

My parents and I waved as the Bauers drove off. It was hard to grin and wave when I was thinking that if their car got stopped and searched, we would be arrested. Even if Hans and Emmy refused to talk, the guards would see our papers inside the wrapped box and quickly figure out that we were preparing to escape.

"Let's get some sleep," Vater said when we got inside.

I was afraid I couldn't sleep without Max, but I was so tired that I dropped off immediately. I had a confused dream in which Emmy was trying to sneak Max into the West Berlin zoo, and I was eating cake while I watched to make sure the police didn't catch her. In the dream, the living room clock kept striking the hour— but instead of going *bong-bong* in its stately way, it chimed shrilly and insistently.

Then I woke up and realized that I was hearing not the clock but the telephone. I heard Vater say, "Hello, Herr Klenk here."

I sat up in bed, wide awake now. Perhaps it was a friend of the Bauers', calling to say they'd been caught!

After a pause, Vater said in a stunned voice, "Oh, no, it can't be! What happened?"

I threw back the bedclothes and ran into the hallway, where the telephone was. At the same time, Mutter came out of the other bedroom, tying her robe around her. We clasped hands. Both of us were trembling.

"Do you think the Bauers got caught?" I whispered.

"I don't know."

Vater was silent for a minute, the receiver up to his ear. Finally, when I thought I couldn't stand it any longer, he told the caller, "Wait a minute." Then he put his hand over the lower part of the receiver, turned to us, and said, "Opa Fritz had a heart attack this morning. He died at the hospital in Freital."

7

MY PARENTS SAT AT THE TABLE FOR OVER AN HOUR, drinking Western coffee and whispering. I sat with them, but mostly I listened.

The phone call, Vater said, had been from Emil Schaefer, a friend of Opa Fritz's whom we knew from our visits to the farm. He'd said that Opa Fritz had had a heart attack early that morning while he and the other harvesters were working in the fields. Herr Schaefer was using the telephone in the post office, which was the only phone in the village and was always available for emergencies.

"Emil said he'd been trying to reach us all day," Vater said. "First we weren't home, then he couldn't get a connection, then we didn't answer. That was him calling this evening when we came in with the Bauers."

So while I'd been shopping and talking to Petra and Ulrike, Opa Fritz had been dead. Opa Fritz! I could picture him as clearly as if he were right there in our living room, with his tanned face, heavy nose, and gray eyes, and his favorite old blue cap covering most of his neatly clipped silver hair.

"I told Emil that we'd notify Adelheide," Vater said. "She won't be back in Munich until next week, and there's no way to reach her before then. We can call her when we get to West Berlin and give her all the news at once. She may be able to catch a quick flight to come visit us and Oma for a day or two."

By the time their coffee cups were empty, Mutter and Vater had made two big decisions. One was that Vater would catch a morning train to Alt Mittelheim so he could go to Opa Fritz's funeral and take care of any business that needed tending to. The other was that when he came home, he would bring Oma with him, if she agreed to come. She would live with us in West Berlin. I would share my bedroom with her, and my parents would put the baby in theirs.

"Do you think she'll come?" I asked.

Vater said, "I think so. She has always said she would want to live with us if anything happened to Fritz. Besides, I don't think she'll want to stay over here when all her family is in the West."

He continued, "Opa Fritz's funeral will be on Saturday, if the arrangements can be made by then. Oma and I can catch a train back here on Sunday morning. Then we'll go West like we'd planned, just on Sunday afternoon instead of Saturday. I'll tell the Schaefers and Oma's other neighbors that she's coming to visit us for a week or two so we can talk things over and look at options for her future."

Mutter sighed. "This is going to be hard for Oma. If she wants to go West with us, she'll have only until Sunday morning to get used to the idea and get ready. She'll hate lying to her friends, too, telling them she'll be back when she knows she won't be."

"I know," Vater agreed. "I wish we could wait a few more weeks to leave, to give her more time to prepare. But we can't wait any longer. We have to leave this weekend."

"Do you really think the border will be closed so soon?" I asked.

Vater hesitated. "I don't know. But even if it isn't, we must go now or we'll lose the apartment. Our deposit will hold it only until the middle of the month, which will be next week. I can't afford to start paying rent on it until we move over there and I can begin getting my full salary in Western marks."

I nodded. The East German government allowed

border crossers to receive just 40 percent of their wages in West German marks; the rest had to be in East German marks, which were worth a lot less.

"And I'll feel better if we're settled in the West before the baby comes," Mutter added. I was sure she was thinking of that pregnant woman who'd died because her husband was a border crosser.

They talked a while longer, and then Vater stood up. "Let's try to get some sleep. There's nothing more we can do tonight."

"Will you be all right, Mutter?" I asked anxiously. "While Vater's gone, I mean."

"I'll be fine. The baby isn't due for another two weeks."

Vater said quickly, "Annemarie, if you think there's the *slightest* chance that the baby's coming, go to the West Berlin hospital right away. Heidi, you help get her there."

"I will, Vater," I promised, picturing myself delivering Little Franzi on the subway.

I fell asleep quickly. The next thing I knew, the morning light was coming in between the slats of my window blinds. I heard the soft *ssshhh* of rain falling and the eerie hoot of a dove. Automatically I reached for Max, and felt an empty space where he usually was in the mornings.

Of course, I reminded myself. Max had gone West.

How funny to think that he was already over there! He didn't know that Opa Fritz was dead.

"Opa Fritz is dead," I whispered. The words shocked me.

My clock said a quarter to nine. As I was putting on my plaid bathrobe, I heard Vater's voice, low and quiet, coming from his and Mutter's bedroom. Then I heard Mutter moan loudly.

I ran to their doorway. Vater was sitting on the edge of the bed beside Mutter, who was lying down with the comforter over her. I'd never seen my mother look like that! Her face was as white as the pillowcase, her hair was uncombed, and her eyes were glazed with pain.

"What's wrong?" I cried.

Vater turned around. "We think the baby may be coming."

"*Now?*"

Mutter moaned again, and Vater patted her hand. "You should be in the hospital," he said.

"You'll have to take me there and go on to the farm," Mutter said, so softly I could hardly hear her. "Oma is expecting you."

"No," Vater replied firmly. "I'm not going to leave you. If you or the doctors needed me, it would be hours before I could get there."

"But Oma—" Mutter stopped and cried out in

pain. I could see how hard she was squeezing Vater's hand.

Vater rubbed his face wearily. I knew what he must be thinking. He desperately wanted to stay and look after Mutter, and she needed him to be here. But someone had to go to Opa Fritz's funeral and, more important, bring Oma back to Berlin.

An idea landed in my head.

"*I'll* go to the farm! Vater, you stay with Mutter, and I'll go to Opa Fritz's funeral and bring Oma back."

"No, Heidi!" Mutter said fretfully. "Karl Franz, don't let her. She's too young."

"I'm thirteen," I told her. "I can do it."

I went over to the bed and lowered my voice to a whisper. "You two go on to the hospital and stay in the West. Oma and I will join you there on Sunday."

Vater pursed his lips, considering.

"You just said last night that we have to go West this weekend," I argued. "The only way we can do that is for me to go get Oma."

"I don't know, Heidi." Vater was shaking his head.

I said, "The trip down there will be easy. The transport police won't bother me, because I'll be going *away* from Berlin and the border crossings. On the way back, we can tell them the truth—that Oma's a widow and is coming to live with us. We just won't say that it will be in *West* Berlin. After we get here, we'll simply get on a subway or city train and go across to the West. I can say I'm taking my grandmother from Alt Mittelheim to visit our relatives in West Berlin for a few days."

I could see Vater wavering. I had one more argument to try. "We're talking about *my* grandmother and *my* mother. I want to help, and I have a *right* to help. If you don't let me do this, I'll feel terrible. Besides, I loved Opa Fritz, and I think that at least one of us should be at his funeral."

Vater looked at me solemnly. "This is a big responsibility," he whispered. "You can't let *any*one suspect we're going West. Even though your mother and I will already be over there, the government could hold you and Oma as hostages, to make us return."

"I understand," I told him.

"All right, then. You start packing, and I'll call the train station."

"No, Karl Franz!" Mutter protested. "She's only a child."

Vater replied calmly, "She's thirteen, Annemarie, and she has a good head on her shoulders. Besides, like she said, Oma will be with her for the trip back. They'll be fine. Oma may be old, but she's a brave, resourceful woman. She'll take care of Heidi."

I started to tell him that I didn't need to be taken care of, but I stopped myself. I didn't want to say anything that might cause him to change his mind.

Vater gave me the small brown suitcase he'd planned to use. I took it to my room, and pulled underclothes and pajamas out of the wardrobe drawers. For the trip, I'd wear my green cotton skirt and the matching striped blouse. My navy blue dress would have to do for Opa Fritz's funeral. It was a little heavy for summer, but it was the only dark dress I had.

Vater called the train station, then came into my room. "I reserved a seat for you on a train leaving at twelve-fifteen," he said. "When you're ready, come into the kitchen and we'll talk."

"Okay."

I finished packing, then dressed quickly. When I went into the kitchen, Vater was making tea. I sliced some bread and spread margarine on it, then took the cup of tea Vater gave me. We sat down at the dining table, and I read the train schedule he'd jotted down: I would arrive in Dresden at three minutes after four, and have six minutes to catch the train to Tharandt. It would stop at Freital at four twenty-three; I'd get off there and have five minutes to catch the train to Alt Mittelheim. I would reach Alt Mittelheim at ten after five.

"I'll call the Alt Mittelheim post office and get a

message to Emil to pick you up at the station," he said. "On Sunday, you and Oma will come back through Riesa instead of Dresden. I'll ask Emil to take you up there. The train leaves at six in the morning. I know that's early, but you can stay on the same train all the way back, which will be easier for Oma. Remember, when the two of you get to Berlin, you mustn't come back here to the apartment, or even to this neighborhood. The neighbors might already suspect that your mother and I have fled West, and it would be dangerous for you to come here."

I nodded, thinking of the Weppelmanns and the rumors that they were retired government spies.

He wrote something else and gave me that piece of paper, as well. It said, "Adelheide Klenk" and had an address in the Wedding District, in north central Berlin.

"This is our new address," Vater explained, "but if the border police find it, you must tell them it's where your aunt Adelheide lives, and that you're going to visit her for the day. Copy the address for Oma, because it will be best if the two of you come West separately. Tell her to tell the border police that she'll be visiting her daughter for a few days.

"Now," he continued, "I've looked at the maps to figure out the best way for you and Oma to come West once you get back to Berlin. Let me show you."

Vater opened a small, colorful map of the Berlin trains and subways.

"Here's the East Berlin train station," he said, jabbing a finger at the little dot. "You and Oma will arrive here on Sunday. Oma will get on this subway line, the red one. Tell her to take it over to West Berlin and get off at the Zoo station. That will be easy for her to remember. You'll get on this blue line, then once you're over the border, you'll change to the green line. Take it to the Zoo station and meet Oma. I'll try to be there, too, to meet both of you. If I'm not there, take this orange line here up to Leopoldplatz. It's the stop closest to our new apartment. Understand?"

I nodded, but I felt as if my head were full of colors, place-names, and instructions.

"Take this map," he said, folding it, "and show Oma what you're both going to do. Don't talk about it once you're on the way home, and don't mark the map. And of course you'll need to use some common sense. If you get here and think these routes seem dangerous, find other ways to get across. The main thing is to get to West Berlin safely."

"We will," I promised as I took the map from him. "If anything goes wrong with Mutter, you'll let me know, won't you?"

"Yes, I'll call the post office in Alt Mittelheim and

have someone bring you a message. If you don't hear from us, you can assume that everything is okay."

He went to take Mutter a cup of tea. I wanted to walk around the apartment and say goodbye to everything: the bow window where I'd sat when I was little, the worn green sofa, the scratched dining table and blue-checked place mats, the beige wallpaper with its pattern of pale flowers—all the little things that made this apartment my home. But I spent five minutes looking for my umbrella, then Vater came in to give me some cash and further instructions, then I thought of some more things to pack, and then I went to visit Mutter. She made me promise to take along something to eat on the train, so I spent ten minutes fixing a cheese sandwich and a thermos of tea. Suddenly it was eleven-thirty, and I had only enough time to kiss my parents, grab my suitcase, and take a final, quick glance around the apartment.

"Goodbye, home," I whispered.

And then I remembered Petra. Goodbye, Petra, I thought, and almost cried. There was no time left for me to make up with her.

Vater walked me downstairs to the front door.

"I'm proud of you, Heidi," he said, and gave me a kiss on my forehead. I hugged him, and he patted my back and said, "You're a brave girl. See you on Sunday."

"See you on Sunday," I repeated.

I hurried to the Bernauer Strasse station, took the subway to Alexanderplatz, and caught a city train to the main station. When I got there, I stood on the platform feeling lost. Where was the ticket office? I had always followed my parents before.

"Upstairs," I said to myself, and ran to the escalator. By the time I had gotten my ticket, it was ten after twelve and I had to ask a porter to help me find the train to Dresden and locate a second-class car.

"Is this your first trip alone, Fräulein?" he asked, smiling, as he handed my suitcase up to me.

"Yes, it is," I admitted, and thanked him for helping me.

Few people were going to Dresden, so I got a second-class coach compartment to myself. I put my suitcase on the rack over the seats and sat down by the window. Soon the conductor blew his whistle and the train slid out of the station.

East Berlin looked bleak in the midday drizzle—all black and white and gray, like a television show. As we left the city, I saw the Müggelsee in the distance, dull silver under the clouds. At least I'd never have to go *there* again.

The buildings became fewer and farther apart, and after the train stopped to take on passengers at the

Blankenfelde stop, we turned south into the country-side.

Once the conductor had come into the compart-ment and punched my ticket, I rested my head on the seatback and watched the familiar landmarks go by: the evergreen woods right before Neuhof, the pretty church spire near Golssen, the little viaduct we went under at Hohenleipisch, and the swelling of the flat land into rolling hills between Uckro and Walddrehna. I'd never see them again!

I wondered when I would next see any farmland or villages. West Berlin was like an island in the mid-dle of Soviet-controlled East Germany. After we had moved, we would be surrounded by East German coun-tryside—and as defectors from East Germany, we could be put in prison if we were caught there.

We made a brief stop at the Elsterwerda station, then crossed the Black Elster River, which wasn't black but pale blue. After that, I ate my cheese sandwich and dozed off. When I woke up, it was a quarter to four and we were getting close to Dresden.

The Dresden train station was smaller than the East Berlin one, but it was bustling, noisy, and impersonal. I felt very much alone as I searched for my next train. I'll be at the farm in another hour, I told myself. But both Berlin and Alt Mittelheim seemed a million miles away. I even wished Mutter and Vater were with me, and I was disappointed in myself. I had thought I would be so confident!

I found the train to Tharandt and settled into a seat. Just a few weeks ago, I thought, I would have given anything to be making this trip. But how different things were from the way I had imagined! I was going to the farm not for a vacation but for Opa Fritz's funeral, Mutter might be having the baby at that very moment, and I had to get Oma and myself to West Berlin to join my parents. I'd never see my home again, and I'd fought with Petra. Right now I didn't even care about Ulrike; I just longed to see Petra. Would I ever get to tell her that Opa Fritz had died, or that I'd gone to the farm, after all?

It was a short ride to Freital. The little half-timbered station there was so small that even I couldn't become confused. I went to the platform out back, at the track to Alt Mittelheim, and waited until the little, black, smoke-belching engine with its mail car and two passenger cars pulled in. I was the only passenger to board.

The train *chuff-chuff*ed through the outskirts of Freital and made its way through the countryside. Soon we were passing the fields of Opa Fritz's cooperative, and Alt Mittelheim itself was just up ahead.

8

TALL, GRAY-HAIRED HERR SCHAEFER was at the station to meet me.

"Your father called the postmistress to say that you'd be coming instead of him," he said, taking my suitcase. "She cycled over to the house to bring me the message."

"Did Vater say anything else?" I asked anxiously.

"He said to tell you that everything was fine, and that he and your mother were just leaving for the hospital."

Even though I knew that Vater's message had been sent hours ago, probably right after I had left for the station, it made me feel better.

Herr Schaefer continued, "He said that Sophie might go back with you to Berlin on Sunday and visit for a while. I asked her if she'd like to do that, and assured her that my wife and I would take care of the farm while she was away. She thought it over and decided she'd like to go. Your father said he'd made reservations for both of you, so I'll take you to the Riesa train station early Sunday morning."

"Thank you," I said.

Herr Schaefer put my suitcase in the trunk of his little white Trabant. As we drove to the farm, he told me about Opa Fritz's death. "He collapsed while he was helping the harvesters in the field. A couple of the workers took him to the hospital in Freital, and I followed them in my car with your grandmother. She talked to Fritz for a few minutes. Then, soon after she left the room, he had another heart attack and died immediately."

"Is he—I mean, is his body at the farm?" I hoped it wasn't.

Herr Schaefer shook his head. "He's laid out in the chapel at the cemetery. The funeral will be there on Saturday. Some of the church ladies prepared the body yesterday, and your grandmother met with the undertaker to make the arrangements." He sighed. "We're going to miss Fritz. He was a good friend and a hard worker."

We crested a hill and drove up to the old brown stucco farmhouse with the beautiful flower garden in front. When my family came for vacation, Oma would watch for Opa Fritz's car to pull up, then come running joyfully out the door to meet us. She'd stretch her arms wide to give us each a big hug. "I thought you'd never get here!" she'd say. Then she and Mutter and I would walk into the house with our arms around one another, chatting and laughing, while Vater and Opa Fritz got the suitcases from the car.

Today when Oma came out the door, she was tearful. Her eyes were red-rimmed, and little wisps of her gray hair stood out around her face. She looked thinner, too; her old flowered housedress hung loosely on her.

"Heidi!" she cried. "Come here, child, and let me hug you."

It was like hugging a frail little bird. Had she gotten smaller? I wondered.

"To think that you came all this way by yourself!" she exclaimed. "You're growing up so quickly. Was your trip all right?"

"It was fine." Suddenly my eyes filled with tears. "Oma, I'm going to miss Opa Fritz so much!"

"So am I, sweetheart, so am I."

Herr Schaefer said, "I'll take the suitcase upstairs, then go see to the livestock."

"Thank you, Emil," Oma said. "Heidi, come inside and have something to eat. I want to hear all about your mother and the new baby that's on the way." She added, "Perhaps a soul is being born to replace the one that has just departed."

"Maybe so." I didn't know what else to say. I had never been to church and wasn't sure how I felt about souls.

There was so much food in the kitchen! On the table were three loaves of bread, wrapped in a checked towel, a chocolate cake, and a fruit torte. The icebox held a platter of sausages, a pork roast, a plate of cabbage rolls, and bowls of potatoes, dumplings, and gravy.

"Oma, you didn't make all of this, did you?"

"No, the women have been bringing in food." Oma set two plates on the table. "There are some things I don't like about the cooperative, but I can't complain about the people. They're so kind and thoughtful! I don't know what I would have done without them over the past two days."

She heated up some sausages and cabbage rolls. While we ate, I told her about Mutter and the baby, and we talked about Opa Fritz and about what Oma would do now.

"I hope you'll come live with us," I told her. "Vater said you might."

She said, "That's what I'm planning to do, if you'll have me. I'll be going back to Berlin with you on Sunday to visit for a couple of weeks. Then I'll come back down here to pack up my things and say my goodbyes. It may take me a few months, but I'd like to move to Berlin before it snows. I don't want to spend the winter here alone."

"Oma," I said slowly, "there's something I have to tell you. You see—"

"Oh, there's Emil at the back door! Would you run let him in?"

I got up to let Herr Schaefer in. While he and Oma talked about a small problem with one of the cows, I sat at the table and fretted. I needed to tell Oma about going West!

There was no chance to talk that evening. Herr Schaefer was still there, and some other neighbors came, bringing more food, and stayed to talk. Oma went upstairs to comb her hair and put on a nicer dress. When she came back down, she fixed tea for everyone, and I passed around slices of torte. I wanted to stay awake until the guests had gone, but soon my head was nodding and my eyelids were heavy.

Oma said softly, "Why don't you go on up to bed, sweetheart?"

"I guess I'd better," I admitted. It was all I could do to wish everyone good night, visit the outhouse, and climb the stairs to my bedroom.

My room was so familiar and welcoming that I

would have cried if I hadn't been so sleepy. Nothing had changed from previous summers: African violets bloomed in homely clay pots on the windowsill, their frosty pink flowers brushed by the short lace curtains; the bed was made up with the old blue eiderdown and pillow covers that matched the stripes on the wallpaper; the wavy mirror inside the oak cupboard made me look squat and pear-shaped; and the picture of Aunt Adelheide, trim and smiling in her stewardess uniform, sat in its permanent place on the desk that Opa Fritz's grandfather had made.

I opened my suitcase, put on my wrinkled pajamas, and hung my other clothes in the cupboard. Then, as I always did at the farm, I cranked open my window before getting into bed. I pulled the comforter over me and fell asleep listening to the crickets and frogs and smelling the sweet scent of the hay that Opa Fritz had helped harvest.

When I woke up Friday morning, the cows were lowing softly and my window was a gray square that dimly lighted the room. I'd forgotten to ask for a clock, so I didn't know what time it was, but I was sure it was much earlier than I got up at home. Still, when I heard Oma go down the stairs and into the kitchen, I decided to get up and have breakfast with her. It might be the only chance we'd have to talk privately.

Oma was surprised to see me.

"Why, Heidi, I thought you always slept late like a city girl! I was going to have tea and bread with butter and preserves, but I can fix you some eggs if you'd like."

"No, that's okay. I'll have the same as you."

"Tea?" Oma asked. When I nodded, she got two cups from the shelf, a green one for herself and for me the pink one with the golden sheen that she knew was my favorite cup.

I took the cups over to the table, and Oma brought the teapot. I looked out the open kitchen window to make sure nobody was around. Then I sat down at the table across from Oma and said softly, "I got up early so we could talk about something."

"Oh?" Oma put down her teacup and gave me her attention.

I said, "Mutter and Vater and I are going West, and we want you to come with us. Will you?"

Oma took a deep breath and let it out. "Your mother told me last year that you might go West someday, so I'm not surprised. I never thought I'd out-live Fritz, but now—yes, I would like to go West and be with my family. I thought it over yesterday, before you arrived, because I thought you might ask. When are you planning to go?"

"That's the thing we need to talk about." I hesitated. "You see, Mutter and Vater are already over there."

"But you mean just to have the baby, don't you?"

"No. I mean for good."

Oma's eyes widened. "For *good*? They've already gone?"

I explained about Vater's job offer and the apartment that was waiting for us, and how our plans had been changed at the last minute by Opa Fritz's death and then Mutter's labor pains. "If you'll come West with us, it will have to be right away—on Sunday, when you and I get back to Berlin."

"Sunday!" Oma shook her head. "I can't be ready by Sunday. There's far too much to do. I need to go through my things and decide what to take—not just clothes and such, but family papers, jewelry, photographs. I need to make arrangements for the house and the animals. Besides, there's Fritz. Who'll look after his grave? Who'll visit it and tend it when I'm gone?"

"His friends will," I replied. "He had so many friends in the village his grave will never be neglected. And I'm sure the Schaefers will continue caring for the farm."

"But all my things—the family papers and such." Oma looked bewildered.

"I'll help you go through them. You'll have to hide them, though, and you'll only be able to take a small suitcase. We can't do anything that might make the border police suspect us. Vater said that if they catch us trying to go West, they could hold us as hostages to get him and Mutter back, and then put us all in prison."

Oma whispered something to herself. I heard God's name, but I didn't know whether she was praying or cursing. She got up and stood at the window, looking outside at the farmyard and barn. Her shoulders shook, and I knew she was quietly crying. I gave her a minute, then went and stood beside her.

"I thought I'd have a few more months here," she said, wiping her eyes with the corner of her apron. "Perhaps I could join you over there later."

"My parents believe the border will be closed," I explained. "They've heard things on the television and radio that make them certain. If it's closed and you're still over here, you won't be able to get West, and we won't be able to come East to see you again. Neither will Aunt Adelheide. We could be separated forever! Besides, it'll be easier if you come now, with me." She looked so sad I put my arm gently around her shoulders. "I understand how you feel. I just found out about it myself a few days ago, and I'm having to leave my life behind, too. It would make me feel a lot better if you'd come with me, so I can be sure I won't lose you as well as everything else."

We stood there silently for a while.

Finally Oma said, "I need to think things over. Let's eat breakfast first. Then, if you don't mind, I'll spend a little time working alone in my garden. That's what I do when I need to think."

"I don't mind," I assured her.

While she was in the garden, I got a bucket of water from the outside pump, then washed the dishes. I dried them and put them in the wooden cupboard, and went out to the barn to visit Marta. Her brown eyes studied me solemnly as I patted her sleek neck. "Thank you for all the rides you've given me," I told her, "and for being a good horse to Opa Fritz. I'll come see you again before I go."

I went from the barn over to Opa Fritz's vegetable garden. My throat ached as I saw the little wooden markers with his faded handwriting. He'd planted this garden last spring, never dreaming that the plants would outlive him. I picked a few late-growing heads of lettuce and some cucumbers to take inside.

It was nearly noon when Oma came back into the house. I was in the kitchen, heating sausages and potatoes for our lunch.

"I've made my decision," she said.

I turned off the burner under the pan of sausages. "What is it?"

"I'm coming with you."

I hugged her. "I'm so glad!"

She returned my hug. "My life here has been a good one, but I'm too old to live here alone, and I can't bear the thought of never seeing my family again."

As we ate, I told her Vater's plan: how we'd cross Berlin separately and meet in the West at the Zoo station.

"Yes, that's a good plan," she said. Now that she had made her decision to come with us, she seemed stronger—less wispy and fragile. Maybe it was because she had a new purpose, I thought. She was looking forward instead of back.

She seemed to read my mind.

"I remember during the war," she mused, "when I got the telegram that Dieter had been killed. I thought my life was over. I guess *that* life *was* over. But a new one began when I married Fritz and moved here. Now this life is coming to an end, and I'm going back to Berlin to begin yet another new one." She gave me a tiny smile. "Perhaps I'll be like a cat and have nine lives."

"I hope so," I replied.

"I only wish I didn't have to leave my flower garden," Oma said sadly. "I'll at least cut the best blooms for Fritz's funeral. You can help me this evening. I'll ask Emil and Irmgarde to come over tonight and take them to the chapel."

That afternoon, the house was filled with people:

the Schaefers and several other couples from the cooperative; Opa Fritz's brother and his family, from their town north of Karl-Marx-Stadt; the minister of Oma's church; and a big, stolid man named Herr Arnold, who sat with Oma, Opa Fritz's brother, and me at the kitchen table to explain East Germany's inheritance regulations.

The farm—the house, barn, gardens, and livestock—belonged to Oma, Herr Arnold said, but only as long as she lived there and was part of the cooperative. If she moved to Berlin, it would go to Vater, but only if he moved here and agreed to become part of the cooperative. If he didn't, the farm would become the property of the government, and the cooperative's board of managers would decide what to do with it.

"I think Emil and Irmgarde would like to buy it," Oma told me later. "They'd like to live on a farm instead of in the village."

I was glad of that. I liked the Schaefers, and they would take good care of the farm.

When the neighbors had gone home and Opa Fritz's relatives had gone to their rooms at the village inn, Oma and I had supper. Then we went out to cut flowers for the funeral.

While Oma was snipping off spires of ivory, pink, and lavender delphiniums, I thought of something. "I know how you can have some of your garden in the

West," I told her. "We'll gather seeds and take them with us, then plant them in our new garden in West Berlin."

"What a clever idea! I left a lot of the dead blossoms on the plants to dry into seeds. I'm sure we can find some that are ready."

We took seeds from the old marigold, zinnia, and sunflower blooms and wrapped them in foil.

"I'll hide them with the family papers," Oma said. "I know how to do it."

After the church ladies had picked up the armloads of blooms, Oma and I began the task of looking through her cedar storage chest. She wanted to take her Bible with the family tree on the inside cover and some photographs of the farm, Opa Fritz, Opa Dieter, and Vater and Aunt Adelheide. I put the photos in an envelope and labeled it "To Show Adelheide," so if the border police saw it, they would think Oma was bringing them to show her daughter in the West.

"If they find the Bible," Oma said, "I'll tell them I read it every night and don't know whether Adelheide has one."

After going through her jewelry box, she decided to take only what she could wear—the diamond wedding ring from her first marriage, the plain gold band from her second, and a locket with an old, faded picture of Opa Dieter in it. She set aside the family papers.

"Is there anything you want to take for yourself?" she asked me.

I considered. "My favorite cup. The pink one. May I have it?"

"Yes, you may. Isn't there anything else you want?"

"No, that's all."

Before we went to bed, Oma and I wrapped the cup carefully and put it in her suitcase. How strange to think that the next time I saw it, I would be in our new home in the West!

The next morning, the people who were going to Opa Fritz's funeral all met at the farm. We were to walk slowly down the road to the cemetery chapel in a funeral procession. As I put on my dress, I wondered what the funeral would be like. I had never been inside a church or chapel. In East Germany, it wasn't against the law to attend religious services, but the practice was discouraged. In the Pioneers, we were taught that we should work for what we wanted, not pray for it. Besides, we were told, religion would take time and energy away from building our perfect society.

"It will be a long procession," Oma said to me as I helped her into her lightweight black coat. "Fritz would be proud."

I walked beside her, with one hand on her arm. She wept into a handkerchief, but her back was straight and her steps never faltered. As we grew close to the chapel, the bells tolled slowly for Opa Fritz and tears began to roll down my face. Frau Schaefer, walking behind us, touched me on the shoulder and gave me a white cotton handkerchief.

When we got inside the chapel, I saw Opa Fritz's plain wooden coffin at the front. It was closed and adorned with a wreath of roses. On the floor in front of it sat vases of the delphiniums, zinnias, and cosmos from Oma's garden, as well as flowers that other people had contributed.

The chapel was cool and dim, and was simply furnished with wooden pews, an altar covered with a white cloth on which candles and a small cross sat, and a wooden lectern where the minister stood. The ceiling was arched, as were the deep-set windows cut into the side walls. The minister said a few things about Opa Fritz, then talked about God, heaven, and being saved. I didn't know whether or not I believed him. I could hear my Pioneer leaders saying scornfully, "It's just superstition—something for the old folks!" but I liked the soothing voice of the minister and the sense of peace I felt in the little chapel. Maybe, I thought, I'd try going to a church in West Berlin someday. Petra would be so surprised when I told her. Then I remembered: how would I ever again be able to tell Petra anything?

After the service, we walked to Opa Fritz's grave site. Two of Opa's nephews, Herr Schaefer, Herr Arnold, and two other men carried the coffin. At the grave, a man Oma whispered was one of the cooperative's managers made a speech about how hardworking Opa Fritz had been and how much he had contributed to the success of the cooperative. Then Herr Schaefer talked about his long friendship with Opa Fritz and what a fine man he had been. The coffin was lowered into the grave and, with a shaking hand, Oma tossed in the first handful of dirt. Opa Fritz's brother tossed in the second one.

After the ceremony, the villagers prepared to walk back to the house.

"I'd like to stay here alone for a little while," Oma told Herr Schaefer and me. "Emil, could you come pick me up in about half an hour?"

Herr Schaefer promised he would and, as we left, asked the minister to keep an eye on her. I wondered if she wanted to whisper our secret, about moving West, to Opa Fritz.

Some of the villagers came back to the house for tea, but they left soon after Oma got home from the cemetery. It was very quiet when they had gone. Oma and I had a small supper, then went upstairs to finish preparing for our trip.

"We need a hiding place for the papers and seeds,"

she said. She took an ivory-colored skirt from her wardrobe and looked at it critically. Sadly she murmured, "I should wear black out of respect for Fritz, but my black skirt doesn't have a lining."

"Why do you need one with a lining?" I asked.

"You'll see in a minute," she said, opening her lingerie drawer. "Get my scissors, will you? They're in my sewing box, on the dresser."

When I returned with the scissors, she was unfolding a white slip. To my surprise, she cut a large, neat square out of it. After she'd put the ruined slip in the bottom of the drawer, she sat down at her sewing machine with the skirt and the square of fabric. While I watched, she stitched the bottom and sides of the square into the underside of the skirt lining, so that it made a big pocket.

"We had to hide a lot of things after the war," she explained as she put the papers in it. "When the Russian soldiers came into Berlin, they stole our jewelry, watches, candlesticks—everything! I hid our valuables in a hole in the backyard."

"And you hid Aunt Adelheide in the cellar, along with a friend's daughter," I added. Oma had told me many stories about those horrible months in 1945, when Berlin was awarded as a prize to the Soviet Union, and the Berliners were at the mercy of its savage, drunken troops.

"That's right." Oma nodded. "They both caught colds and were nearly blinded by the sunlight when they came out, but that was far better than what would have happened if the Russian soldiers had gotten them."

She made sure that the soft old papers wouldn't rustle, then added the foil-wrapped flower seeds and sewed down the top of the pocket. From the outside, you couldn't tell there was a pocket in the lining.

"We'd better pack our suitcases and get ready for bed," she said. "Emil will pick us up at five to take us to the station."

We soon had our small suitcases packed and sitting in the hallway. I went over the plans again with Oma, showed her the subway map, and gave her our new address. Finally, we decided we were as prepared as we could be. I went to the outhouse and stopped by the barn to say goodbye to Marta. Then, for the last time, Oma and I went to bed in our rooms in the old farmhouse.

9

THE NEXT MORNING, Oma and I got up before sunrise, sleepily ate breakfast, and washed the dishes. At a few minutes to five, we were in the hallway, waiting for Herr Schaefer. When we heard his car coming down the road, Oma burst into tears.

"I've had a good life in this house," she said, sobbing.

I hugged her, but I was in tears, too, and didn't know how to console her.

"You'll like it in Berlin," I said. "We'll have a garden, and you can go to church."

She pulled a handkerchief out of her purse and dried her eyes. "I know, sweetheart. It'll be a fine life. It's just that I can't believe this one is over."

"I can't either, Oma."

Herr Schaefer knocked on the door, and Oma took a deep breath and went to open it.

"Good morning, Emil," she said, composed again. "We're ready to go."

"Is this all your luggage?" he asked in surprise as he picked up her little suitcase.

"Yes," Oma answered smoothly. "I'll get the rest of my things when Karl Franz brings me back."

As we drove away, Herr Schaefer turned on the radio, but nothing happened. "It must be broken," he said apologetically after twisting the volume and tuning knobs. "I was going to see what the weather forecast is for Berlin."

"It looks like it will be a sunny day here," Oma commented.

At the train station, Herr Schaefer parked the car and carried our luggage through the small building and onto the platform. Soon the Karl-Marx-Stadt–Berlin train pulled in, its black engine huffing and spewing smoke like a great dragon. We found a second-class car, and Herr Schaefer got us settled into an empty compartment.

"We'll see you in a couple of weeks, Sophie!" he said.

Oma smiled and said, "Yes, Emil. I'll let you know my schedule." After he left the train, she whispered to me, "I wish I could have told him the truth."

There were no stops and few towns on the route to Berlin. Oma lowered the shades in our compartment, and we dozed off. Several times I was awakened by people opening the door to our car and walking down the corridor outside Oma's and my compartment. Once a woman cried, "Have you heard the news?" and a man replied, "You mean about Berlin? Yes, it was on the radio earlier. I can't believe they . . ." Then the door on the far end of the car opened and closed. What news? I wondered, vaguely uneasy. I dropped off to sleep again, and woke up when the train was rolling through the outskirts of East Berlin. Oma was awake and looked at me worriedly.

"The people in the next compartment are crying," she said.

I listened, and heard sniffles and sobs. They seemed to be coming from more than one person.

"I suppose it's not my business to go ask what's wrong," Oma said, sounding as though she might do it, anyway.

Just then the loudspeaker crackled, and a man's voice said, "Your attention, please! All passengers should note that certain restrictions have come into effect regarding the public transportation system in Berlin. Please read the instructions posted at the station."

Oma and I looked at each other, puzzled. A minute later, when a conductor came into our car, Oma pulled back the door to our compartment and said, "Excuse me, sir. Can you tell us what that last announcement meant?"

He replied, "Some of the stations on the border were closed last night, ma'am."

"Which ones?" I asked. If they included the ones that Vater had said Oma and I should use, we'd have to change our plans quickly.

He looked at me a moment before he answered. "Virtually all of them, Fräulein, unless you have the correct papers."

"What papers do we need?" Oma asked.

"You must ask at the station," he said, and continued down the corridor.

"Maybe he just meant our identity cards," I told Oma. But my heart was pounding, and I could see the anxiety in her face.

I opened the window shades. As we approached the Warschauer Strasse station, the one before the main station, I saw a sight that chilled my blood: Soviet tanks were spread across the street, facing the bridge over the Spree River to West Berlin. Soldiers were putting a machine gun into place.

I caught my breath. "Oma, something's wrong!"

She looked past me out the window, and I heard her whisper the same prayer or curse she'd used before. When the train pulled into the main station, we grabbed our suitcases and got off with the stream of other passengers.

Everyone around us looked as bewildered as we felt.

"They've closed the border!" someone cried hysterically.

"It's just temporary," someone else said. "Look, there's an announcement posted on the wall. Maybe it will explain things."

Along with the others from our train, Oma and I hurried over. But the small, dense print on the announcement was hard to read, and even harder to understand.

"Listen," someone said excitedly, and read: " 'The city train station remains open at Friedrichstrasse as a connection to and from West Berlin, but the trains now begin and end on platform B.' So we can get through! It's only certain platforms that are closed."

We went up the escalator and got onto a city train. It was crowded, and a young man gave Oma his seat. I stood next to her, holding on to a pole. Like the people in the train station, the passengers looked confused and frightened. A few cried. One woman kept saying, "I'm sure it's all a misunderstanding. There *has* to be a way across."

We got off at the Friedrichstrasse station. It was packed with people: some cried with frustration; some milled around in confusion, tightly clutching their bags; and some sat resignedly on their suitcases, waiting to be told what to do. Guards, soldiers, and police were everywhere. I had never seen so many uniforms! A line of black-clad transport police blocked the stairs to the upper level. Border guards in light-brown uniforms and broad helmets and East German police in their familiar light green coats stood watching. They were silent and grim-faced, one hand on the submachine guns slung over their shoulders. Civilian fighting groups, trained to protect East German factories, strode through the station in their gray overalls. Riot police, East German soldiers, and firemen in black uniforms and army helmets hurried through the crowd on their way to trouble spots.

Oma and I pushed through the people, toward the front of our train. A high barrier, made of wood and barbed wire, had been built across the tracks so that it couldn't go any farther.

"How do we go West?" I asked, baffled.

A transport policeman turned to grin at me. "You don't, Fräulein! Not anymore!"

I felt frantic sobs building up inside me.

"There must be a way over," Oma murmured, patting my arm. "The announcement said platform B, remember? Let's go there."

We held up our identity cards to the police at platform B, but they just pushed us back along with everyone else who was trying to get through. "You don't have the right papers!" they yelled, shaking their heads impatiently.

"What *are* the right papers?" my grandmother demanded loudly.

"Papers saying you are a citizen of the West," one of them answered wearily.

"But we're not citizens of the West," someone cried. "We just want to visit there."

"I'm sorry, but you can't. The borders are closed to everyone except those with Western identity papers. Now get back, please. We don't want to have to hurt anyone."

"Let's go outside and try to find another way over," I said, tugging at Oma's sleeve. "If we get separated, we'll meet at the new apartment if—if we can."

"We'll find a way," Oma said in a low, determined voice. She bent her head close to my ear. "We had best leave our suitcases, though. We'll have a better chance of getting over without them. Let's lose them when nobody is looking."

"But my pink cup is in yours!" I protested. "And all the photographs!"

"We'll have to leave them," Oma said firmly.

The platform was so crowded with tearful, bewildered people that it was easy to set down our suitcases and walk off without them. I put mine near the station wall, knelt, and pretended to tie my shoe. Then I straightened up and walked away empty-handed. I didn't see where Oma left hers; she just suddenly didn't have it anymore.

Goodbye, pink cup, I thought.

Outside, there were tanks and soldiers in the parking lot beside the station. East German police barred the way to the entrance to the subway line. A truck with loudspeakers went slowly down the street. "Stay calm!" came a voice from the speakers. "These protective measures are being taken for the good of the people." Rocks pelted the side of the truck, and two policemen ran past Oma and me, yelling, "Stop!" as they chased the rock-throwers.

I clutched Oma's hand. "I'm scared."

She squeezed my hand in reply. "I know. But there must be a way over. Let's walk to another station."

We walked south down Friedrichstrasse to the Französische Strasse station. The metal grillwork across the entrance was closed and padlocked. Policemen stood guard.

Oma sighed. "Let's go on to the next one."

The next station, a few blocks south, was also closed.

Oma said, "Before we go any farther, let's find a place to sit down and eat something. Perhaps we can learn what's going on."

We walked around until we found a small café. Since it was between breakfast and lunchtime, few people were there. A young waitress with short red hair and a kind smile showed us to a table by the window and brought us menus. I just shrugged when Oma asked what I wanted. How could I think about food right now?

Oma ordered a late breakfast of sausage, cheese, rolls, and tea for both of us. "And please," she asked the waitress, "can you tell us what's happening? We've just arrived from Riesa on the train."

The waitress replied, "The government closed the border during the night. The city trains and subways have stopped going West, and barbed wire fences are being put up between East and West Berlin so that people can't cross by foot. People say that the barbed wire will be replaced by a wall."

"A wall!" Oma exclaimed.

"Herr Ulbricht said that nobody was going to build a wall," I said.

The waitress shrugged. "He says now that it's being done for our own good."

In an innocent voice, Oma asked, "Isn't there anyplace where people can still cross? We came to visit relatives in the West. I hate to simply turn around and go home."

"All the crossing places have been barricaded." The

waitress leaned closer and dropped her voice to a whisper. "But I have heard customers say that there are places where the fences aren't finished, where you can walk through the gaps or step over the coils of wire when the police aren't looking."

Two men came into the café just then, so she left to show them to a table behind us. Oma and I looked at each other. I knew we were thinking the same thing: we'd have to look for one of those places where the barriers weren't finished.

Someone turned on the radio that sat on the counter, but it gave us little news—just smug, joyful announcements. "Our self-protection measures are proceeding as planned! Soon an anti-Western barrier will be in place to keep the peaceful citizens of the East safe. Then we can build our ideal socialist society without the interference of the West!"

One of the men who had just come in said, "The Americans won't stand for this. We'll have a war now, for certain."

The other man replied, "They can't do anything. The barrier is a few feet inside East Berlin. The Americans can't keep our government from putting up a barbed wire fence—or a ten-foot wall if it wants one—on its own land."

A man at another table turned to them. "The Americans don't have the *right* to do anything. This is our country, and I'm glad Herr Ulbricht is putting up a wall. If we want to build a socialist society, that's our business. I'm tired of the Americans trying to tell us what to do."

The woman with him nodded. "That's right. I'm tired of those snobby West Berliners, too. They come over to get their hair done and their TVs repaired because it's so much cheaper here than it is in the West—and then *we* can't get appointments."

The waitress brought our plates, tea, and tableware, then set our breakfast platter and a basket of rolls between us. I put some food on my plate, but I only nibbled at it.

"Eat, Heidi," Oma urged in a low voice, pouring tea into our cups. "We must stay strong. That's one thing I learned during the war. If you're weak with hunger, you can neither think clearly nor act swiftly. And we will need to do both today!"

I nodded. My stomach hurt and my throat was so tight that I could hardly swallow, but I tried to imitate Oma as she calmly and slowly ate her half of the breakfast.

When we'd finished, Oma paid and we used the ladies' room. As we left the café, the radio was playing a march that I remembered hearing at Pioneer celebrations.

Dark clouds were covering the sun, and the temperature had dropped a little. Where would we go if it rained? How strange to be in East Berlin—my home! —and have no place to get out of the rain.

Oma murmured, "Let's walk toward the border and see if we can find one of those weak points. We'll pretend we're looking for a friend's house."

"Do you have a plan?" I asked.

"I'm working on one."

We strolled leisurely down Friedrichstrasse, chatting and pretending to be interested in the store window displays. Because Berlin was divided not straight down the middle but rather by a crazy zigzagging line, we were headed toward the border with West Berlin even though we were walking south. Soon we began to hear the ugly sound of jackhammers tearing up the pavement. It got louder and louder until it seemed to rattle our bones.

"They're putting in posts to hold up the barbed wire fence," Oma said, pointing. At the intersection of Friedrichstrasse and Zimmerstrasse, soldiers were shoving a post into a raw wound in the pavement while four border guards carried a huge roll of barbed wire over to them. Two East German policemen patrolled the street, watching both the sad, silent little knots of East Berliners and the jeering crowds of West Berliners who had gathered on the other side.

"Hey, guards!" one Westerner taunted. "What are

you doing—making East Berlin into a concentration camp?"

"Yeah!" cried another. "If socialism is so great, how come you have to put up barbed wire to keep your people from leaving?"

"Is this your ideal society?" someone yelled.

So quietly I could barely hear her, Oma said, "I think those policemen are mostly worried about barricading the intersection. They may have left the work on Zimmerstrasse unfinished. Let's see if we can find a weak spot there."

One of the policemen, a tall, helmeted man with a bayonet fixed to his rifle, came up to us as we approached Zimmerstrasse.

"Let me do the talking," Oma whispered to me.

"You cannot go any farther, ladies," he said firmly, fixing us with eyes that were as hard and gray as his steel helmet.

I started to turn away, but Oma cried indignantly, "What do you mean I can't go any farther? I've come all the way from Alt Mittelheim to visit my friend Waltraude Grossenfelder! She lives on Zimmerstrasse, and she is expecting my granddaughter and me to come for lunch."

The policeman shook his head. "I'm sorry, but you cannot go onto Zimmerstrasse unless you live there."

Oma stuck her chin in the air. "*I* don't live there,

but *Waltraude* does and she's expecting me. She was the maid of honor at my wedding, and we haven't seen each other for fif—teen—years!" She jabbed her finger at him as she said it. "We went through the war together and we're both widows now, and I have come all the way up here to see her, and I *will* see her."

"I'm afraid I can't allow that."

"You *must* allow it!" Oma raised her voice even louder. "Waltraude's son is *very* high in the government, and he will be furious to learn that you have kept his mother's oldest friend away from her! He *knows* how much Waltraude and I have been looking forward to this day, and he will want to speak—personally—to—you!" She jabbed her finger at him again.

A crowd of people was gathering.

"Let the old lady go see her friend!" someone shouted.

"You have no right to abuse elderly women!" someone else cried.

The policeman glanced at them nervously. To Oma, he said, "Well—all right, but I shall have to escort you."

"No, no!" Oma pretended to misunderstand. "I'm not so old that I need an escort."

"It's not because you're old, ma'am—"

"I'll be just fine. My granddaughter will escort me. Now, young man, you had best get back to your partner. He's having trouble with those hecklers across the fence."

The policeman murmured, "Yes, ma'am," and rejoined his partner as Oma and I started down Zimmerstrasse.

"Oma," I whispered in awe, "that was terrific! You weren't scared at all."

"Oh, I was scared, all right," Oma replied, "but I learned something after the war. We were all scared of the Russian soldiers, but we found out we'd be safer if we didn't show it. Often they would leave us alone if we bullied them. And," she added with a little smile, "I did have a friend named Waltraude Grossenfelder who was in Dieter's and my wedding."

As we'd hoped, Zimmerstrasse had coils of barbed wire lining its southern edge, but no fence had been put up yet. Oma and I sauntered casually along the northern side of the street, pretending to look at the street numbers on the buildings. We kept an eye on the policemen who were patrolling the area. They had a long stretch to guard, and soon they turned their backs.

The moment they did, Oma said, "Let's cross the street. Maybe we can get some Westerners to help us."

We walked over to the coils of wire. They were only about knee-high.

"Can someone help us?" Oma called softly to the

West Berliners who were gathered on the other side. "Please! We must get across to our family!"

Two strong-looking boys exchanged glances and ran over to us. "We helped some other people earlier," one of them said. "Put your foot up on the wire, ma'am. We'll lift you across, then the girl."

Oma tossed her handbag over, and put a foot up on the coil of wire. As quick as anything, one of the boys lifted her and set her down on the other side.

She was over.

"My!" She gasped. "Now it's your turn, Heidi. Hurry!"

I put my foot up on the wire. A boy reached for me, but my skirt got caught on a barb and pulled me back. "Wait a second," I said, and bent to free myself. It was difficult because my hands were shaking so badly.

"Hey! Get away from there!" a man shouted.

I whirled around. Two policemen were rounding the corner onto Zimmerstrasse, reaching for their submachine guns as they ran.

I screamed and stepped backward off the coil of wire, nearly falling. One of the policemen fired a shot into the air. I heard Oma scream, "Heidi! Oh, my God, Heidi!"

I ran down Zimmerstrasse. I could hear the horrified West Berliners crying, "Don't shoot! She's only a child!" and "Someone stop them! Help the little girl!"

I ducked into the next side street and ran, through alleys and down sidewalks, between apartment houses, and around piles of rubble left from the war. I ran until I thought my lungs would burst.

Finally I slowed to a walk, and when I was sure the policemen were no longer following me, I sank down on the doorstep of an apartment house on a quiet back street. I was shaking all over. My skirt was torn, and my leg was bleeding where the barbed wire had scratched it.

"I've lost them," I whispered to myself. "They won't find me. I'm safe now."

But even though I was safe, I was still in East Berlin.

10

WAVES OF PANIC WASHED OVER ME, making me tremble and sob uncontrollably. East Berlin, my home, was
suddenly terrifying—just like the Müggelsee the time
I'd nearly drowned. And, as I had in the Müggelsee, I
felt small, helpless, and very much alone. I had wanted
to be more grown-up and independent—but now I
wished desperately that my parents or Oma were here
to help me.

There must be a way across to the West, I thought.
It became a chant in my head: *There must be a way, there
must be a way.* The rhythm of the words was soothing. I
sat on the doorstep and rocked myself gently to it.

If Oma were in this situation, I thought, she would
make another plan. So I made one myself. I didn't dare
go near Zimmerstrasse again. Instead I would walk
north and look for a place to get across the barbed wire.

If I hadn't found one by evening, I'd catch a city train and go to our garden. It wouldn't matter if people saw me, because I often went there on Sundays. I had enough money left over from my trip to buy the train ticket, and I had the keys that Vater had given me. I could spend the night in the cottage, which had cots, running water, and electricity, and I could pick vegetables to eat. Tomorrow morning I'd try again to go West. I'd be rested then, able to think more clearly.

I felt better now that I had a plan.

The western end of busy Leipziger Strasse was blocked by tanks and police, so I couldn't reach the border there. I walked up another block and turned left onto a side street, which came out at Ebertstrasse. There the barbed-wire fence bordered the Tiergarten Park, where a crowd of West Berliners had gathered to protest. I went up close to the fence, waved my arm, and cried out, "Are the Klenks there? Does anyone know Herr Klenk at Sterns's Auto Shop?"

People shook their heads. Disappointed, I turned to leave. An East Berlin policeman watched me suspiciously.

"The police are nervous," I heard a man tell his friends. "Someone cut a hole in the fence a little while ago, and about fifty people got across, right over there."

I looked at where he was pointing, and saw workmen repairing the barbed wire. If only I had come earlier, maybe I could have escaped, too!

Since the area around the huge Brandenburg Gate was closed off, I went back to Friedrichstrasse and walked north. In the parking lot beside the subway station, a group of Pioneers and Free German Youth had gathered. "Our government is always right!" they chanted in unison. "Hooray for Herr Ulbricht, our leader!" Several girls wearing jaunty red Pioneer scarves were taking sodas, snacks, and flowers to the soldiers who stood beside the army tanks. I watched, disgusted, as the girls smiled and made little speeches to the men. Then, as the girl nearest me turned around to walk back to her Pioneer group, I saw who she was. Petra! Suddenly I was as angry as when she'd lectured me to please Ulrike. I didn't want to make up with her anymore.

She saw me at the same time, and waved. "Heidi, wait!" she called. I turned and walked swiftly away, but I heard quick footsteps behind me and soon felt a hand on my shoulder.

I whirled around. "How could you do that?" I whispered fiercely. "Smile and tell those soldiers they're heroes?"

"I had to," she whispered back. "All the Pioneers have to do it. You would, too, except that you weren't home this morning. Frau Hoffmann sent me over to look for you, but nobody came to the door."

"Opa Fritz died," I told her. "He had a heart attack a few days ago. I just got back from the farm."

"Oh, I'm so sorry, Heidi. I know how much you loved Opa Fritz." Petra looked around. "Let's find someplace to talk. And don't run off again! I need to tell you something, and I have to meet my parents in a little while."

The best place we could find was a deserted alley, behind some trash cans. It was smelly, but private.

In a low voice, Petra said, "I'm sorry I talked to you about your father the way I did. I know he's a good person and that you're proud of him."

"Are you saying this just because I told you he has a job in the East now?"

She shook her head vehemently. "No! I'm saying it because even while I was talking to you that day I felt phony and awful. You see, my father and Ulrike had both been going on and on about how your father was selfish and unpatriotic, and they said it was my duty to talk to you. I guess I heard them say it so much I started to believe it. I finally promised I'd talk to you. But then when I did, I hated myself. I didn't blame you for getting angry." She made a face. "I sounded just like Ulrike, didn't I?"

"I thought Ulrike was your friend," I said in surprise.

Petra shrugged. "Only because my father insists on it. Her father is his boss now. At first I thought she was pretty nice, but then I realized she just wanted somebody to show off to. I have to admire her diving and her artwork, and listen to her brag about how she runs the Pioneers. Hmmph! It's a good thing she's going off to camp soon. Otherwise I'd strangle her, even if my father would kill me for it."

Slowly I said, "I'm sorry I didn't give you a chance to explain things earlier. I *was* thinking of coming over the day after I saw you on Brunnenstrasse, to see if we could talk things out. But then Opa Fritz died, and I had to leave for the farm."

In the parking lot by the station, a Pioneer choir began singing.

Petra fervently whispered, "I hate all this! All this smiling and singing and saying, 'Friendship with the Soviet Union!' and 'The party is always right!' over and over. Inside I'm thinking about how we'll never get to go to West Berlin shopping or to the zoo again. And the poor people who have friends or family in the West! I see them waving to each other, and my heart aches for them. I think this barrier is *horrible*. Be glad—well, I can't say 'Be glad your Opa Fritz died.'

But be glad you have an excuse not to join in the *festivities*." She said the word bitterly.

I was silent, thinking hard. I had promised Vater that I wouldn't tell Petra about our going West. But he had also said to use my common sense—and my common sense was telling me that I needed help and that I could trust her to help me. Besides, now that the border was closed, she wouldn't be able to come West to find me. I *couldn't* leave her without saying goodbye!

I whispered, "Petra, listen to me. I'm one of those people with family in the West."

"You mean your aunt Adelheide?"

"Yes, but not just her. My parents and my grandmother, too. They've gone West."

"They've gone . . . ?" She shook her head slowly, not understanding. "But you said—you just got back—and your father has a job here—and . . ."

Quickly I told her what had happened.

"So you're leaving," she said flatly. "We may never see each other again."

"I can't think about that right now," I said, feeling my chin tremble. "If I do, I'll sit down and cry, and I'll *never* get over to my family. Look, Petra, I need you to help me. If you don't want to, I'll understand. But I'm really desperate."

She looked pale and scared, but she swallowed hard and said, "What do you want me to do?"

"I need to know where to try getting across. Has your father mentioned any places where people are still escaping?"

"No, but he was talking earlier about how soon the barrier will be finished. I can ask him if there are still any places where someone could get through. I'll say I'm just curious."

"Can you ask him today?"

"Yes, I can ask him while we're at home this afternoon. I'll meet you later and tell you what he said." She thought for a moment. "How about four o'clock in the park where we weeded the flowers? I can tell my parents I'm going to a Pioneer activity."

"Thank you, Petra! You're saving my life."

I hugged her, and suddenly neither of us could hold back the tears any longer. We clung to each other and cried until a truck with its loudspeakers blaring went past on Friedrichstrasse and startled us.

Petra brushed away her tears with one hand, and said, "I'd better go find my parents now, before they start looking for me. I'll see you at four."

"Okay. And bring me some shorts or slacks if you can. This skirt's hard to run in."

After she left, I wandered around for a while. People mostly stood in little groups, talking quietly and glancing anxiously about. Near the Tiergarten, a band was playing marches. Nobody stayed to listen, though, because close by stood ten army tanks, three of them with their guns lowered and ready to shoot. The music was nearly drowned out anyway by the *ratta-ratta-ratta* of the jackhammers and the roar of the heavy trucks along the border.

At twenty minutes before four, I went to the Friedrichstrasse station. The stairs leading down to the subway were so packed I couldn't even get in. I sighed and set out walking to the park. It was a couple of miles and I didn't arrive until after four. Petra was already there, wearing her Pioneer uniform and carrying a shopping basket.

"My parents went out, so I was able to gather up some things for you," she said, holding out the basket. Inside it were a thick bread-and-margarine sandwich, a bottle of soda and a bottle opener, a wet washcloth, and some dark blue school gym shorts. "The cloth is to clean the scratch on your leg."

"Thank you," I said gratefully, and wiped the dried blood off my leg. "I didn't dare go back to our apartment for anything. I was afraid our neighbors might have notified the police that we'd gone."

A ghost of her old grin visited her face. "They hadn't this morning. I was over there, and your door wasn't sealed off, but guess whose was—the Weppelmanns'!"

"You mean the *Wep*pelmanns went *West?*" I stared at her, astounded.

"There was a big red seal on their door."

"Ha! Here I was so afraid they'd hear my radio, and all the time they were planning to go West, too!"

"It looks that way," Petra said. "Now sit down and eat while I tell you what I found out from my father."

I ate the sandwich and washed it down with soda as she whispered her information to me.

"I asked my father—very casually, mind you— whether there was any place that people were still escaping. He said that a lot of people had gotten across at Bernauer Strasse. They ran through the back door of the apartment buildings and out the front door, or jumped out the front windows onto the street below."

I nodded, picturing it. On Bernauer Strasse, at the northern edge of our neighborhood, the apartment buildings themselves formed the border: they were in the East, but the street in front of them was in the West.

Petra continued, "It's a lot harder to get across there now, because the police are keeping people away. They won't let you near the street unless you can prove you live in one of the apartments along it."

"It was like that at Zimmerstrasse this morning," I

said, shuddering. "I don't want to go through that again."

"I didn't think you would. Although," Petra added slowly, "I don't think you'll like the alternative any better."

"What is it?"

"Well, my father said that people are still getting across by swimming the Spree River or the Teltow Canal. He said some guards are stationed at both, but not enough to patrol the whole length of them all the time."

"The canal's near our garden," I said slowly. "But you can't be suggesting . . ."

"That you swim it? Yes, I am. You're a good swimmer, and the canal's not very wide. I looked it up on a map—it's only fifty meters. You've swum that far before, lots of times."

"But only in a pool, where I could stop and rest if I needed to! Besides, I haven't swum at all since—well, you know."

"Heidi, you have to stop thinking about that!" Petra urged. "Swimming the canal is the best way to get over to the West, and tonight may be your last chance. My father said that by tomorrow there will be more policemen guarding the canal and the river. There are going to be underwater barriers, too, as soon as they can be made and put into place."

I stared at her. I was going to have to swim across the Teltow Canal tonight. *The Teltow Canal!* I shivered as I thought of how it would be: *The dark, cold water would close around me and I'd panic. I'd scramble frantically, trying to touch the bottom with my feet, but I wouldn't be able to reach it. I'd choke on the water and cough. The guards would hear me splashing and choking and they'd shoot at me . . .*

"Maybe I'll just spend the night in the cottage," I said, "then look for a weak place in the fence tomorrow."

"Tomorrow will be too late, Heidi! My father said the work crews will be out all night. He said that by tomorrow morning East Berlin will be totally fenced in with barbed wire, and then the crews will start putting up a wall where the fence is."

At that moment a loud voice interrupted us. "What are you girls doing here?"

We both jumped. A policeman was standing on the sidewalk, looking sternly at us.

"We—we're just talking, sir," Petra said.

"Well, you'd better be getting home. It doesn't look good for people to sit and whisper on a day like this. Someone might think you were plotting something."

He sounded so pompous that on any other day we would have had a hard time fighting back the giggles.

Today we just muttered, "Yes, sir," and obediently stood up. He walked on, but we knew he was nearby, watching us.

I tucked the blue shorts under my arm, and gave Petra back her shopping basket. We quickly hugged goodbye. Petra whispered, "Take care of yourself!"

"You, too." I thought for a moment and added, "Tomorrow, go to the edge of the Tiergarten at noon. I'll be there, too, on the Western side. And thank you again, a million times!"

"I'll be thinking of you," she said, and was gone.

I left the park, feeling lonelier than ever.

For the next two hours, I trudged along the border, trying to find weak spots. It was the same everywhere: the barrier was firmly in place and guarded. By evening, I was exhausted and discouraged. Petra was right: the only way to get West was to swim.

Wearily, I got on the city train to go to our garden. When we stopped at the main train station, I thought of how long it seemed since Oma and I had arrived there. Why, just this morning I'd awakened in my bedroom at the farm!

After I got off at the stop near our garden, I studied the map on the station wall and planned my route to the canal. I would have to be very careful: the canal made a sharp angle, so that it formed a sloppy sideways V. Tonight, as I walked from our garden to the canal, I would reach the upper leg first, and cross the bridge over it. I'd still be in the East until I got to the second, lower, leg. That was the one I had to swim across to reach the West.

Nobody was working in the gardens that day, even though the sun was out. I unlocked the door to our garden cottage and went inside. The spiderweb I'd left untouched on my last visit was gone now. I wondered whether even the spiders had fled West.

I took off my green skirt and pulled on Petra's gym shorts. They were a little tight, since she was skinnier, but at least my legs were no longer encased in the skirt.

It wouldn't be dark out for a few hours yet. I tried to take a nap, but even though I was exhausted, I was too excited to sleep. Finally I got up, took the trowel and clippers from the shed, and went to work in the garden. Working would calm my nerves.

I wondered what would happen to our garden. Would Herr Hartz take it over? I hoped so. He was a good gardener, and he would be glad to have the extra food. I knew that Vater had given him a key to the gate. I didn't know whether he had a key to our cottage, as well, and thought of tossing mine over the fence into his garden before I left. But, no, I decided, I might need it again if my courage failed me when I reached the canal.

After I had clipped and weeded for a while, I picked

a couple of tomatoes and washed them at the sink inside the cottage. I sat on the front step and ate them whole, like apples, while I gazed at the garden. How I was going to miss it! I wished I at least had a photograph of it. An idea struck me. I could take some flower seeds West, to add to the ones from Oma's garden!

I gathered bunches of dried marigold heads, which would break apart into seeds. After a lot of hunting, I found a plastic bag in the cottage to put them in, and added my identity card and the cash left over from my trip. I tucked the bag inside the waistband of Petra's gym shorts and secured it with a safety pin that was in my purse.

Finally the sun set behind West Berlin. As I watched out the cottage window, the sky dulled and darkened. It was time to go.

"Goodbye, cottage," I whispered, locking it behind me. "Goodbye, garden."

If I was lucky, there would be only one more goodbye: to East Berlin itself. Then I could start saying hellos.

As I made my way to the canal, a chorus of evening frog songs rose from the wide, swampy Heidekamp ditch on my right. Once I heard a radio playing in someone's house. "Herr Ulbricht is delighted," the newscaster was saying. "Everything went exactly as planned. The Westerners suspected nothing!"

I crossed the bridge over the upper leg of the canal, and left the houses behind. Out here, the entire area was made up of rented garden plots and cottages, with unnamed alleys dividing the rows. Smells of garden soil and dank canal water filled the night air. There was no moon. The black sky had a pink tinge from the glow of the city, but the only points of light were a few streetlights and, here and there, a lamp in a cottage.

It shouldn't be much farther, I thought. I began shaking as I considered what lay ahead of me.

Suddenly, up ahead, I saw bright lights moving around and heard voices. The border guards! Quickly I ran down the nearest alley and ducked onto a tiny path between gardens. I hid behind an unoccupied cottage for a little while, then made my way back to the road. But in which direction should I turn? For a moment, I panicked. Then, in my head, I pictured the map at the Plänterwald station. The main part of the city was to the north. So if I was heading west, the pink glow in the sky should be on my right side.

I turned left and started down the road. Even though there weren't any more voices or moving lights, I walked silently, like a ghost in the night. After a long time, I reached the end of the garden zone. I sensed a drop-off ahead and heard water lapping. It was the canal, and there were no guards or rolls of barbed wire between me and the water.

The steep bank was covered with goldenrod that shone dimly in the darkness. I walked carefully, my arms outstretched for balance. Once I fell and grazed my knee, but finally I was at the canal's edge. I wasn't tired anymore. My heart raced and my hands trembled.

"Goodbye, East Berlin," I whispered.

Quickly, before the guards came by on their patrol, I took off my shoes and hid them down in the goldenrod. I put my keys inside one of them. My clothes were nearly as lightweight as a swimsuit, so I kept them on. I wasn't going to arrive in West Berlin wearing only my underwear! Besides, the plastic bag was pinned to the waistband of the shorts.

I walked into the water until it was around my ankles. The opposite bank seemed miles away. Petra said it was only fifty meters, I thought. All I had to do was swim fifty meters, and I could go home to Mutter, Vater, and Oma.

I wondered whether Little Franzi had been born. It was funny—I didn't resent the baby anymore. My new brother or sister would be part of my family, another Klenk to love.

I took several deep breaths, then walked into chest-high water. There was no side to push off from, as in a swimming pool, so my first strokes were slow and awkward. I panicked, and churned the water wildly until I found the canal floor with my feet. By then I had splashed so much, I knew that every border guard in East Berlin must have heard me. I had to get across quickly.

"God, let me cross safely," I whispered. I still wasn't sure I believed in religion, but I had to ask *someone* for help.

As soon as my heart stopped racing, I set off again. This time I got a better start, and felt myself gliding through the water, my arms making smooth, powerful strokes.

I'm swimming, I thought in surprise. *I'm swimming and I'm not scared of the water. I can make it across!*

Then, as I turned my head out of the water to breathe, I saw people running down the bank ahead of me, waving flashlights. They shouted, but I couldn't hear what they said.

A horrible thought hit me. Perhaps I'd gotten turned around when I'd been running through the gardens, and was swimming back across the first leg of the canal! If so, the bank I was heading for was still in East Berlin—and those people could be border guards who had figured out that I was trying to escape.

My heart pounded with terror. I swam on, because there was nothing else I could do. I couldn't stop here, in the deepest part of the canal, and I was far too tired to swim back to the other side. Besides, the border guards might be waiting for me there, as well.

More people were clambering down the approaching shore, and the flashlights made a blinding glare on the water. There was more shouting. I heard people yell, "Fräulein!" but all their other words were muffled by the water. My arms and legs were weak from fatigue, and I swallowed some foul-tasting water as I turned my head to breathe. But I had to keep going.

Finally I sensed that the muddy canal bottom was close under me. I tried to stand up and found that my feet didn't yet reach the bottom. But then I heard splashes, and suddenly it didn't matter that the water was over my head, because strong arms were lifting me. The people on the bank were shouting again, and now I could hear their words clearly: "Hooray, Fräulein! You made it! Welcome to West Berlin!"

Epilogue:
Three Days Later

SOME FRIENDLY WEST BERLINERS GAVE ME dry clothes and shoes to wear, and others invited me to have dinner with them or spend the night at their home. People took my picture, told me how brave I was, asked if I needed a doctor, and even pressed Western money into my hands. I felt like a heroine! Mostly, though, I wanted to be with my family. When a cab driver offered to give me a free ride to our new apartment, I gladly accepted.

The Bauers were spending the evening with Vater and Oma, who were sick with worry. Mutter wasn't there; she was in the hospital with my baby brother, Franz Dieter Klenk. Vater used the Bauers' phone to call the maternity ward and have a nurse tell her that I was safe.

Our new apartment has no refrigerator or telephone yet. The only furniture is two beds and a sofa, and all our towels, sheets, dishes, and blankets have been loaned by the Bauers and Sternses. But our clothes and papers got here safely, the clock says our names from its new shelf, and Max smiles sweetly from my makeshift bed on the floor of Oma's and my room. Tomorrow, Mutter and Little Franzi will come home. I met him at the hospital yesterday.

He was by far the cutest baby in the nursery, and I was proud to be his big sister. As I watched him sleeping, wrapped in his tiny blue blanket, my mind raced with plans. Someday I would tell him about my escape, and about the farm and Opa Fritz and Petra. I'd help him learn to walk and read, and I'd teach him how to garden. I'd give him swimming lessons, too!

Monday morning, I went to the Tiergarten to meet Petra, as we'd planned. I waited near the barbed wire for nearly an hour. At last I saw her, hurrying up the sidewalk on the other side of the street, wearing her Pioneer uniform. She looked over and scanned the faces in the West. When she saw me, her face lit up. I could see the relief in her eyes as she ran across to me.

"You made it!" she whispered, thrusting her hands over the wire.

I clasped her hands in my own, mindful of the East Berlin policeman watching us a short distance away.

"Yes, thanks to you," I whispered back. "You were right. It wasn't as bad as I was afraid of. I thought about you thinking about me, and it helped."

I glanced at the policeman. It was hard to talk, with him standing so close and the barbed wire right under my wrists. Petra and I were only a few inches apart—yet we were in different worlds.

"I'm wearing my necklace," I told her, nodding toward the little gold heart that hung around my neck.

"I know. I'm glad. It seems like a long time ago, d-doesn't it?" Her voice broke, and she took one hand away to wipe the tears from her face.

I nodded, knowing she meant my birthday.

She tried to grin. "Hey, when you go to the zoo, say hello to Knautschke and his family for me. Tell them I guess I won't be able to visit them anymore."

"I'll tell them. Oh, and guess what! I have a brother."

"Congratulations," she said. "Is your mother okay?"

"She's fine."

We just stood there for a while, holding hands, trying to think of things to say. But the things we wanted to say had to stay inside our hearts.

Finally Petra squeezed my hands and then pulled hers away. "I have to go. I'm taking Dagmar's place in the Pioneer choir today while she's out with a cold. We have to meet by the Potsdamer Platz at one-thirty, to give a concert for the guards. My parents are going to take photos." She glanced back at the watching policeman, and whispered, "I'm glad I could help you yesterday! It makes me feel better about all this other stuff. Thanking the guards and things. At least I know I did *something* good. But I miss you awfully."

"I miss you, too. Come back tomorrow at the same time!"

"I'll try." She gave me a long last look, then whispered, "Goodbye," and hurried back across the street.

I cried all the way to my new home. Some of the tears were for me, and some were for her.

I went back to the Tiergarten in the morning both yesterday and today, but Petra wasn't there. "Do you think I'll ever see her again?" I asked Vater. He replied, "I don't know, sweetheart. Perhaps it's just as well if you don't try to meet. She has to adjust to her new life, and you to yours." He said it in a kind, gentle way, and I know he was right. But it's impossible to think that Petra and I will grow up and live our lives and get old and maybe even *die* without ever seeing each other again!

Now the work crews in the East have started replacing the barbed wire with a wall—the wall that Herr Ulbricht said no one intended to build. Vater and I went to see the first part of it, which is going up near the Tiergarten. It's an ugly thing, made of concrete blocks, rubble left from the war, bricks, and whatever else the crews can cement together. Not only that, but the telephone service between East and West Berlin has been cut. Soon East Berlin will seem as far away as the moon.

We have heard on the radio that the East Berlin border police are now shooting to kill people trying to escape. At least one person was killed on Monday, only blocks from Zimmerstrasse. And last night two people were shot at, although not killed, as they swam across the Teltow Canal. I don't understand how our dream of building an ideal society has turned into such a nightmare. Vater says he doesn't think anybody understands.

Tomorrow Oma and I are going to buy some pots and soil so we can raise a few flower seedlings inside over the winter. We're going to have a seed-planting ceremony, with her, Mutter, Vater, and me. It was my idea. Each of us will say a few words about what we miss from our old life and what we hope for in our new one. Then we'll each plant a seed in memory of the people and places we love in the East. I know that Oma will say a prayer for them. Perhaps I will, too.

APR   2007

J
Dah

Dahlberg,
Maurine F.,
1951-
    Escape to
West Berlin
